Pardon Our Monsters

Pardon Our Monsters

Andrew Hood

ESPLANADE
Books

THE FICTION SERIES AT VÉHICULE PRESS

Published with the generous assistance of the Canada Council for the Arts, the Book Publishing Industry Development Program of the Department of Canadian Heritage, and the Société de développement des entreprises culturelles du Québec (SODEC).

Esplanade Books editor: Andrew Steinmetz

Cover design: David Drummond
Photo of author: Crystal Porcher
Set in Adobe Minion and Book Antiqua by Simon Garamond
Printed by Marquis Printing Inc.

LIBRARY AND ARCHIVES CANADA CATALOGUING IN PUBLICATION

Hood, Andrew, 1983-
Pardon Our Monsters / Andrew Hood.

ISBN 978-1-55065-232-1
I. Title.
PS8615.O511P37 2007   C813'.6 C2007-904439-5

Published by Véhicule Press, Montréal, Québec, Canada
www.vehiculepress.com

Distribution in Canada: LitDistCo
orders@lpg.ca

Distribution US: Independent Publishers Group
www.ipgbook.com

Printed in Canada on 100% post-consumer recycled paper.

For Matt

Contents

Acknowledgements

Thanks to Andrew Steinmetz for wiping my face clean, straightening my hair, and fixing my shoelaces before sending me off; to Benjamin James Lancaster, Katye Seip, Lorraine Price, Olivier Spénard, and Sara Peters for their early perusals of some of these stories; to Ali Naccarato and James Irwin for throwing me the occasional bone, photocopying me into their respective rags (where a few of the little fictions may have first appeared); to Adrian I.T. Kramer for the gift of *Sky High*; to Ross Lyle for consistently raising the bar out there on the dance floor; to Paul Beer and Colin Browne for playing Adverbs; to Jeannie Taylor for telling me about her hybrid holydays and her riverbank time-passers; to Crystal Porcher for the photo and the patience; to Tim M.M. Kramer, a friend whose mind-boggling cruelty is surpassed only by his mind-boggling generosity; to the McAuslan Brewery for their generous financial assistance during the writing of this book, asking only forty hours of labour each week in return; to Simon Dardick and his tireless posse at Véhicule for taking, I feel, a chance; to my parents for absolutely everything.

Indefatigable gratitude to Trevor Ferguson for caring enough to threaten violence.

"Grant me your pardon," replied the thief, "and I
will tell you the whole truth."

–The Tale of Bakbak, The Barber's Third Brother

A Sound Like Dolphins

THERE'S THIS NOISE that I could do for a long time without stopping, an alarm of boredom that was not always intentional. On restless nights I would drone in long, insect tones from my bed, waking the entire house with this creaking chirp that comes from somewhere between my throat and nose. When I sang this sound on purpose I changed the note by opening my mouth wide like a scream and then tiny, like a smooch. I made little cricket ditties or words that really got under my brother Shannon's skin when I was his shadow during that summer.

"Fuck off with that, will ya? Jesus, Joe, you're just always—"

Shannon stopped asking and charley-horsed me on the shoulder instead. He had those perfect round knuckles and a swift downward swoop to make the hit really smart. Over the past few months he'd gotten strong but it was hard to tell whether he knew it or not. His fist could get through the meat and right to the bone, so more than anything you ached. And an ache's the worst because the throb's there for a day or two, and a bruise won't show until a lot later. When the proof does appear it's a sickly yellow and green circle on your arm.

He delivered a good one, but I didn't fuck off. He was so mean and lovely, my brother. The only affection I could hope to get from him then was specific and personalized violence. Shan knew how to hurt me without really hurting me, like a stage-fighter kicking just millimetres in front of your face so that the only pain you feel is from your own tense anticipation of being hurt.

We passed under the maple in my friend Paddy's front yard and Shan reached up and snatched down a branch without missing a step. One by one, delicately and considerately, he pulled off all the leaves until the stick was naked. Then he snapped it in half over his bare knee, biting his bottom lip as he brought his leg up and the branch down. He made an *oof* sound and puffed out his cheeks.

Like they were bike spokes, he fiddled the stick between my legs and tripped me up. I stumbled and fell on someone's front lawn, scuffing my knees and palms green.

Across the street a man was mowing his yard without his shirt on. He was slim but with this big tanned gut. He saw. He stopped mowing and gave us this look, all cross and with his fist on his fat hip, like if we didn't solve the problem ourselves he'd come over there and solve it for us. Shannon helped me up like we were pals and it was all a big mistake.

"That guy's a fucker," Shan muttered, spitting.

"He's a fucker?" I aped, an eight-year-old slowly learning the language, squawking back in the little girl's voice I had when I was especially excited.

Shan laughed, hearing his words from my stupid mouth. "Yeah. Exactly."

It was the beginning of July and we were going down to swim at the river, taking the long way through the streets instead of cutting through people's backyards. More adults were on vacation then and didn't like looking out their kitchen window and seeing two brothers hopping their fences and stomping around in their flowerbeds. Instead of shorts I'd worn my red trunks, which was fine for the day, but got weird and itchy at night. Shannon had only just grown out of his old trunks, so he made do with a grey pair of Dad's cut-off track pants. Only *NIK* remained in neon green plastic block letters. The summer before we had forgotten our beach towels at Solbol Beach, so we snuck the good purple bath towels from the linen closet and slung them over our shoulders like we were detectives.

We walked in a terrible silence. Without doing it on purpose, I was an insect again, an anonymous chirper in the background of a joke poorly told.

"You're a shit, you know that? Joe, you're embarrassing." Shan was looking off somewhere else, not settling his eyes on any one thing for very long, kind of jittery. He ripped his fingernails off with his teeth and spat them out. "You do that stupid noise and everyone stares, not at you but at me like I'm some fucking nut or something to be walking with you."

Coming up to the sign for the bus stop Shannon wound up with one half of the stick in his right hand and swung it like he hated the metal pole so much. Like everything that was wrong in his life was all because of that goddamned bus stop. The branch shattered, dinging against the metal. He probably felt an angry numbness in his palm, the way you do when you miss the sweet spot on a Louisville Slugger.

He tossed the splintered nub behind him and swung the leftover half around like it was a sword, twirling it in front of him. He made swooping sound effects—*swoosh, swish, sha, sha, shwa*—as if the sword were cutting the hot summer air.

The pretend sword always missed my face. Just. I flinched and hung back. My jaw tingled. Shan was preparing himself for a battle. There would be a war.

His name is not a girl's name, okay. He's named after our grandfather, a man with thick white eyebrows who died in a boxing ring when he was fifty-three and who was named after the longest river in Ireland. Shan's face is strong and Irish, even when he was that young, and his hair is black like a sea that the sun never hits. But just before school got out that summer Shannon sprouted breasts. He had only just turned twelve and was learning how to skateboard, how to tackle a guy without hurting himself, and how to read the signs between a catcher's thighs.

They were these two chubby puberty cones with a few sparse hairs circling the nipples, his boobs. He worried that people were always staring at them, ogling, so he kept his arms crossed tight against his chest, like he was fed up, all in an attempt to suppress those big jiggling shames of his. If I wanted to see him get really sore at me, so mad that he would hold back none of his awkward strength, I would call his breasts tits. Or worse, titties.

Titties, titties, titties, titties, titties, titties, titties. That's the lyrics to a song I wrote that went with every melody. A dance can go along with it too, but doesn't have to.

Hey. Nice tits, fatty. That's what his best bud Stu had said to him that one recess. Shan wound up and popped him right in his stupid nose. He smashed his friend's face and there was blood all over his hand and for a minute after he was calm, amazed by Stu's thick blood, running through his knuckles like his river. It just looked really cool, Shan had told me. He said that if I wanted to see what it looked like he could bop me too, so I had better quit my dancing.

Around the same time he got his breasts—his boobies, his jugs, his boobums, his knockers, his ta-tas or cha-cha's—the White Rabbit folded, leaving its head chef, who happened to be our father, out of work. Then the Board of Education cut its budget and my mother cleaned out her receptionist's desk a few weeks after my father. It was hard on our parents, sure, but Jesus it blew even more for us. It ruined that summer vacation. That summer was supposed to be our time, me and Shan's. The house was supposed to be ours. Instead of cleaning dishes, we'd eat lunch over our bodies. With crumbs in the folds of our lazy guts we were supposed to breathe heavy, get dull and watch TV.

That dream got snatched away from us. Poor us.

It wasn't our parent's fault. I sort of got that. Stuff like that happens. It's not fair and it's not unfair, which is worse. Ugly times are easier when there's someone to blame.

All of our belts tightened at a time when Shannon's waist was expanding. Most of his own clothes didn't fit him anymore, and cash was too scarce for brand new stuff, so he wore Dad's old things. There was that one navy Queen shirt with the big pink bleach stain on the front. *Fat Bottomed Girls, You Make the Rocking World Go 'Round!* was written on the back, the way lifeguards have *LIFEGUARD* on their T-shirts. Like big-boobied Shannon was the fat-bottomed girl or something.

The weather the summer when this was happening was the kind where it feels like there's no weather at all, only a stagnant nothing where everything but the birds is so quiet and you feel like you've got to treat it delicately. Walking in the streets is like breaking into a house, where you've got to be so silent and so careful. At least that's how I felt. I think Shannon felt compelled to fuck it up as best he could, stomping around and knocking over lamps, letting the owners know he was there.

We'd rise up in the morning at the crack of nine and watch the queue of morning shows—Donahue, Sally, *The Price is Right*. Shan liked to watch the war coverage on CNN. The Middle East was all beige and wind. The Iraquis were as poor as we were, wearing clothes from the same period in the '80s. When we got fed up with our parents coming in and out of rooms, we took off, usually staying out until the red dusk when the streetlights were just coming up. Sometime after lunch I would hear Shannon slam the front door and I would up and rush after him. Out of work, Mom and Dad had nothing to do, so they kept busy trying to make the reality of that whole rough patch a little less destructive.

Dust couldn't settle. My mother cleaned the house, singing along with pop songs on the radio, not always knowing all the words and filling those gaps in with her own special brand of muted gibberish. For some reason, from somewhere, my Dad had all this wood lying around in the shed. He got up in the mornings and conceived projects—hatched plans. He spent his days making useless things: entertainment centres and birdfeeders and bookcases with room for more books than we owned. Why buy new things when you can make them? I'd never seen the two of them so proud of themselves. Each time a picture frame got righted or a plank of wood planed and blown clean of its soft, yellow frosting, you'd think that they'd just won a marathon, or shot a rocket to the moon, or something crazy like that. They made the best of the worst.

But Shannon couldn't take it. Nothing was fair. Everything was a weight to be lumped onto his growing back. If he stuck around the house too long he would either get mad at Dad for asking him for help with a project or else he'd start telling Mom to *fuck off* and *go away* when she'd ask him something really simple, like what he wanted for lunch, or what he was going to do that day.

One time, I was upstairs in my room and I heard him shouting with her in the basement, his voice having become so low and terrible. They were fighting over laundry. I wasn't there and can't know why, but he put his fist into the laundry room door and ran out. When I caught up with him in the schoolyard behind our house he was marching, pumping his thick arms. His face was blushing with hot blood and was slick with tears. He kept honking back the snot that snaked down his thin mustache and onto his lip. He didn't say a word but he let me walk with him as he stomped and snuffled, wiping his eyes with the heels of his hands.

Shan had scared the shit out of himself, I think, flipping his lid like that. He hated himself for being what he was and having no control over it. He wasn't mad at our parents. A mood would just take him over and he'd do mean things like that. A second later, it would kill him, cut him in his most sensitive places, when he realized what he'd done. So he kept his distance and I kept my own distance, trailing him everywhere that summer like toilet paper stuck to the bottom of his shoe.

The dent is still there, like a big puckered asshole blowing a kiss, splintered into the wood.

Along the bank of the river that runs through Corbet, there is a spot where young thieves ditch stolen bikes from the summer before. The bikes pile up on the mud in a big rusty heap, and, if you searched long and hard enough, you might be able to ferret out a long lost BMX from three years ago. Not just bikes, though, but other tossed crap like shopping carts and car tires and maybe even a computer, all used up until useless. Owners and thieves no longer wanted the responsibility, so they dumped illegally in the river and dusted their hands clean. The big idea was that no one would ever know because that spot at the river was a secret, quiet place, which is why me and Shan liked it. The trees grew huge on the shore so it sort of felt like you were swimming indoors.

It's important to understand that, in times of war, everyone is an enemy. No one is to be trusted, not even your own brother. As far as Shan knew, I would turn on him at any time. As a precaution, my brother always kept his shirt on when we swam together. As hidden as our spot was, I was still there, and I might whisper into the ear of the World the truth of who he really was and he couldn't let that happen.

It was sad because, with his shirt wet, it only made him bustier. His shirt stuck so sleekly to his skin that you could make out the tits perfectly—two big pointy mountains—and also all those chubby rolls bunched up whenever he bent over. He was always picking his shirt off his skin, pinching soaked fabric, making a *thwack* and *schuck* sound. Swimming with your shirt on, you miss that feeling of really being in the water, feeling your skin in the current and feeling all the little hairs on every part of your body. When you jump in with your shirt on you're not swimming, you're just getting really wet.

There does not need to be a reason, so don't ask. Don't go mining. The rush is over and these mountains have been tapped of all valuable answers. When we walked past our Presbyterian Church, not far from the river, Shan booted over a garbage bin and spilled trash all over the sidewalk, newspaper and McDonald's sacks. Shannon kept walking like he hadn't done anything, kicking one of the Coke cans in front of him. It rattled on the cement. There was still some pop in there, splattering black on the grey sidewalk every time he kicked it.

"Shan, why'd you kick that trash thing over?" I asked him.

To really get a rise out of him I would try to hold Shan's hand.

Maybe his body was so sensitive that he couldn't stand to have anyone touch it. He'd smack my hand away but I'd go for his big paw again. I'd quit it when he called me a queer.

"What do you mean 'why'd I kick it over?'?" He slapped my grabby hand one last time and crossed his arms like a gym teacher. He stopped kicking the can and dangled his shoe over it high and then stomped down like it was a skull. Or, no, not a skull, not that, that's too much. Whatever it was like, it crunched and curled around the sole of his shoe and when he started walking again, the can crackled beneath him.

"Why do you do stuff like that? You're always kicking this thing or smashing that thing. Making a mess. Why're you always doing that stuff?"

You could smell the river before you ever saw it—the smell of moss and mud. And when you got closer, if you made a point of it, you could hear the mumbling of the water and the insects you heard but never saw.

"Why shouldn't I?" He snatched my Jay's cap from my head and held it up high so I could almost get it when I jumped, but couldn't quite. He gave it to me again, acting like someone else had stolen it and he'd just gotten it back for me. I stopped to put it back on, just so, and then ran to catch up to him. His legs had gotten long and strong and he moved really quickly in long strides. He let me walk with him, but he would never wait up for me.

"But why do you though?"

"Just fuck off, huh? Jesus. Why've you always gotta bug me about all these things?"

Decisions were being made, councils were being held without his permission and he had to deal with the consequences. Bullshit. It was all around him like a cloud of summer sweat gnats: you could be frantic and swat at them, but that would accomplish little more than making you look foolish.

The city was doing construction by the bridge and they had just laid new cement. Shannon stopped before going down the hill to the river and looked around to see if anyone was coming. He peeled the can from his foot and tossed it on the road behind him.

"Just nudge me if you see anybody, eh?" He crouched down and with the other half of his stick he wrote *Fuck Saddam* in big, tall letters. His teachers always commented on how beautiful his printing was, and my mom would always comment that they commented. Shannon stood up, looked at it, liked the way it looked, and then handed the stick to me. He had been gripping it so tight, swooshing around his sword, that the bark was warm and moist.

"You write something," he said.

I got on my knees in front of the sidewalk, the block of fresh cement smelled like a just-pissed-in cat litter box. I didn't know what to write. There was nothing I hated enough to put in cement, to have linger and nag forever. Shannon had so many reasons to hate things. Shit was all around him and all he could do was swing blindly—fuck with all the little things. Petty vandalism got to be his only defence. He hated the trees and he hated the garbage cans and he hated the sidewalk—the Blue Jays, being poor, his friends, our parents being home all the time, the glare on the TV, the Gulf War, Saddam Hussein and his big fat titties: everything was to blame. Every bit of it was just one more prick on his already riddled body.

But me, little lame me, I was still dopey and in love with so much. I loved the Blue Jays and I loved swimming in the dirty river and I loved my Mom and I loved my Dad. And, oh man, I loved Shannon. I'd never tell him because he would have socked me, but I just loved him so much. The best were those few seconds where I got to hold onto his hand before he shook it away. The year before, when I was seven and he was eleven—before he got boobs, before we were poor, before the war—I was allowed to hold his hand sometimes and even kiss him every once and a while. And he'd tell me that he loved me too if I said it first. But that all changed when he got tits. It's the hardest thing in the world to love someone who hates themselves so honestly and completely.

The mesh of my trunks rode up my crack. From the ground I looked up at him with my sad dough eyes, my brother so high and fat above me, and said, "I don't know what to write."

With the cool indents of grass on my palm, I stood up next to Shan and we looked down at his *Fuck Saddam*. He bent over, snatching the stick from me, and stuck it back into the cement and stirred it. Finished, he stuck the branch up straight and started down the hill towards the bank of the river, leaving me behind.

I watched him go. He'd gotten so big so quick that his body must have hurt terribly, each bone stretched and tired like he'd been tortured on the rack for information he didn't have and couldn't lie about. All of him limped, gimped, and hobbled. He was a tower about to topple from the strong and fetid winds of a shit storm. I stood by the cement soup as he headed for the water, slowly disappearing in the shade of the willows.

Fat Bottomed Girls, You Make the Rocking World Go' Round!

I got this spark in me then, a feeling that my body didn't want to be still anymore. A feeling that it needed to move, that it would not stand being still, that the world spun only because I walked on top of it. I was a shark, and to be still was to be dead. So I took off like a shot, running.

Shan was a ways away so I ran so fast to catch up. I loved running and I loved moving, hearing the sound of my feet thumping hard and flat on the grass, feeling the beat and rattle all the way in my teeth. I loved going so fast down that incline until it felt like my legs couldn't keep up with the rest of my body, like my short stems would fall out from beneath me if I went any faster. I was testing the limits of what my body in partnership with the dusty earth would and would not allow.

It was like that. I got going so quick down the hill until I was about to fall on my face. But just before that happened I made a huge jump. I sprang, both feet on the ground like it was track and field tryouts, landing and grabbing onto Shannon's back like a newborn palming a grown man's finger, wrapping my legs around his waist and hooking my arms around his big shoulders. I held on so tight and got so close that I could hear his heavy breaths, feel the moistness of his sweaty back and sniff his sour smell. It had been so long since I had been that near to him. I wanted to pull his body inside of mine to keep him safe and give him a soft place to hide out for a while, until the storm calmed.

He stumbled a bit at first, mumbled *fuck*, but got strong again and ran faster through the tall grass towards the river—so fast I could tell that he was getting that feeling too. This was war, where we see who we were, who we are, and who we might be. Let's run into battle. Brother, we will be gusto. Oh brother. Oh man. Oh boy. I felt the thumps of his size twelves thumping in my chest. The willows' spider legs brushed my face as Shan reached around and held my back before he jumped in. I was on him like a backpack. I closed my eyes, freed up a hand to plug my nose and held my breath.

Before mussing the still surface, we hollered this big loud bellow, like we had been swinging from vines. We would not be sneaky about our attack. We'd be balls out, in the air together.

I am young and I am in love. I am small and brave. I will make the first move. I will leap and sail in between it all, off earth and not in sky, and when I do, I will ask you to catch me or let me fall. If you don't catch me, I trust you will provide a soft place to collapse.

Will you allow flight? What will be the limit? Let's discuss, or let's just be silly and ballsy and excited and find out. How elastic is my tether? Because if you give me an inch I will scoot a mile like the wind and learn how to be strong and speedy. I will learn to be strong and speedy and I will show everyone else how. I am small and I am young, and I will try and hold your hand, World, until you smack it away and call me a fag.

We made bubbles like creation, and we sunk like stones. Our bath towels skimmed on top of the river like water bugs. Underwater, I kept hold as long as Shannon let me. In such a short time my brother had become this big, angry, violent thing, who was always so heavy, hairy and pained and whose only defence was pathetic vandalism. But in the water, when I held him—a big loving hug—he felt weightless, like I could lift him up so high with my weak arms. All those things that pissed him off couldn't get at us underwater. We were in a movie, escaping from a swarm of angry bees.

In that smoky brown place I saw nothing and I heard nothing. For that short time I held my breath and I held my brother and everything disappeared. Except there's that noise I get in my ears when I'm underwater. I don't know if it happens to everybody. It's a sound like the chattering and squeaking of dolphins. It's the sound of the entire river pressing on me, trying to get into my body, only my ears are so tight that it can't. The water squeals and squeals, wanting in so bad, but my body will never allow it. But it was so short a time. I could only keep my breath for so long before my lungs started to get tight and I had to let go of Shan and come up for a sip of air.

Chin Music

So. I WAS TRYING TO CUT the devil's throat and Fitz was skipping stones. We were killing time. In the houses on the opposite bank of the Gimlet River, the blunt yellow kitchen lights were blinking out one at a time, to be replaced by the spastic television-blue flicker in the living rooms. Frugh sat behind us on the trunk of a toppled and rotting maple that was half in and half out of the river. She whistled while she prepared our drugs for the evening.

Even just dicking around, skipping stones or whatever, Fitz's athleticism shines. A beacon light, for some, though not for me. His is a refined pitcher's form, accentuated this night by his grey and navy Corbet Monarchs uniform. For reasons I didn't know and didn't care enough to ask after, he was in full regalia that Friday. Lucky number 37—— "The Maestro" as he was dubbed by the Corbet *Mercury*—pivoted onto one foot, brought his knee close to his chest, cupped hands to his heart, peeped over his left shoulder to check the man on first—me—and side-armed his stone, snorting a *hmmf* through his nose. I counted ten skips not counting the dribbles at the end which curled off like the tail of a twister.

Fitz throws smoke.

Each of his failing and bastardly attributes is balanced—though often in a wonky and precarious way—by great talents performed with autistic precision and mindless gusto. No one else I know can put every bit of themselves into a curve ball, a prizeless foot race or a masturbatory sketch of what one of their best girl friends might look like naked quite like Jon Fitz can. That's why I hate him.

I had played catcher and never learned to skip stones. Instead,

I always try to cut the devil's throat, which is sometimes easier, though just as impressive. I'd nailed a toss once before, at camp when I was ten, but never since. And when you've done something once it's natural to assume that you've got the stuff in you to do it again. No one wants to give too much credence to the role of flukes in their lives. I mean I don't. So, fitting a flat, smooth stone in the sickle of my index finger I snapped my wrist and released the stone at the tip. It went spinning above me, out and over the water. If done right the stone will hit the surface with no splash, just a clean cut along the dark and wrinkled neck of the slow devil that meanders through Corbet, Ontario.

My stone hit the water with a messy plop and that devil kept huffing air. I'm not so hot at riverbank games and never pretend to be. I quit trying and took a seat next to Frugh who was just finishing with our popper bottle. She had looked better, if you ask me, when I had first met her in the winter. She had had her comic-book-black hair cut short and tight to her head, like a boy's, giving ample stage time to her slim neck and square jawline. She has a broad jaw like a millionaire. Since then, though, she'd put in tawny highlights and let her hair grow to her shoulders. Now it was always falling in her face.

Fitz hucked another stone and it went *dip dip dip*, sending out shivers along the craters of the harvest moon reflected in the Gimlet. The stone hopped and petered just short of an abandoned shopping cart on the other bank. Fitz started to hoot, going *woo-woo* and dancing his little dance. This is the routine where he waves his palms in the air before he brings them down level to his waist, putting them flat like you would do on the hood of a car if the police had you do it. Except Fitz doesn't pretend a hood. Rather, he has some-one's generous rump in mind. Then his hips start thrusting, his head goes back, and he starts *mmm, mmm, mmm*ing. That's all the dance is. It's more of a performance piece, really.

With Fitz I hold back my chuckles because I don't want to en-courage him. Fitz will cure any and all silences, disturb all still waters. He can't stand nothing happening, so he, himself, will always be happening—going and doing and being. In short, he's an asshole. Frugh looked up from the electrical tape she was futzing with and smirked. Frugh frowns when she smirks, kissing out her lips and narrowing her eyes. I had expected more of her, frankly. Like most girls, Frugh had eyes for Fitz the minute she met him. Now, she was holding back her guffawing because you would never want a guy like that to think he had the upper hand.

"Who's that you're fucking there, Jon?" she asked in a tone both mocking and encouraging.

Fitz's hands started to rove smoothly and wildly over the invisible behind as he sped up his thrusts and bit his bottom lip, seriousing his face. "I'm fucking the world because I—am—so—fucking—great. *Mmm, mmm, mmm.*"

I scowled at him but he only winked back and kept gyrating. Like it had been when we played ball together, Fitz would shake off the signs I flashed him between my thighs just to piss me off.

It was supposed to have been only myself and Frugh. Like it used to be. But Fitz had buzzed my apartment in the late afternoon. He had been drunk, uniformed and insistent that I include him in whatever Friday night plans I had. I figured—a crossed-fingers sort of estimation—that Frugh would be unaffected by Fitz's shenanigans and we could be embarrassed for him together. It would bring us closer together. Instead, she was buying him.

She leaned into me, sniggering behind my back. "That guy's quite a card." She had the chalky, sweet aroma of cheap art-room paints that I'd come to cherish, mixed with a dash of sandalwood.

"You think that's funny?" I smacked at a mosquito humming at my ear.

"Yeah. I do."

"He's just being stupid."

"I know. He's goofing around. I don't know. That's funny. Lighten up. He's your friend, not mine."

Fitz was still fucking air and would keep it up as long as he had an audience. "So what's the score?" he called to us. "Have you covered up the cracks? Are we good to go? How good is the going gonna get?"

Our popper bottle was an empty wine bottle shaped like a sitting cat, the mouth of the bottle growing from the top of the cat's head. Frugh had bought it for me months back as a joke about me hating cats. We had tossed it back together, so I thought that I might convert it into a drug apparatus as a joke about the ridiculous amount of pot the two of us smoked. I had been waiting to hear back from a friend about getting a diamond drill-bit to make a clean, perfect hole for the chamber when Fitz arrived. The Monarchs' summer baseball camp went until six, but there he was, still dressed to play and—I could smell—as stewed as a prune.

He had answered my impatient questions of "Aren't you supposed to be … ?" and "Are you … ?" by hammering a nail into the glass cat's stomach.

"There," he had said. "Perfect."

Lucky for us all, the bottle didn't shatter but there were more than enough cracks snaking out of the hole to make the bottle too draughty and ultimately useless. Fitz's slapdash and slipshod remedy was electrical tape wrapped endlessly around the cat's belly and back like a tensor bandage to ensure an airtight, foggy high.

Frugh bit at the tape with her crooked front teeth and smoothed out the wrinkled bits. She put the mouth of the bottle to hers, covered the loading cylinder with her thumb and sucked in. Nothing. No leaks. She handed it to me to inspect. "That should be all right," she said, blankly, like a physician. "Except there's a lot of tape around the pipe. We're gonna end up burning it and inhaling it."

"Is that bad for you?"

"I'm sure it's not good." Frugh stood with the popper bottle and started up the bank, toward the playground, hoisting and steadying herself on a twisted root. Her blue jeans had a frayed tear just below the crease of her bum. I knew it well.

Fitz was *ooooing* and gyrating now, grunting a little bit. "How're you making out over there?" I called to him.

"The world's super-tight, see …" His breath was short. In all

28

that pump and pomp he was getting a good workout. "So you've gotta fuck 'er super-hard. Let 'er know you're there."

I knew Jon Fitz from baseball. We had played together on the '99 Corbet Select team, catcher and pitcher. If we had gone to school together I would never have talked to him. He has a mesomorph's body that woos women of any age when packaged into a uniform one size too small for him. His head is thick with short curly hair, frosted at the tips and always kept stiff with gel. I suspect that he tweezes his eyebrows too. Chubby boys notice these things about their male friends. Whenever Fitz and I are side by side, women always manage to angle me out of their gaze.

Pitching, Fitz had heat but at the price of control and stamina. The one season I spent on the team was mostly wasted digging his wild pitches out of the dust and making the futile throw to second or third. Home was stolen constantly. Call him on it after games and he'd balk jokes and excuses back at you, loud enough for everyone else in the locker room to hear.

"Naw, Matters, you've got it all wrong. Man, I've got great control. I just like to see you hustle and move a bit. You're getting too doughy squatting there all game. You're starting to get the body of a first baseman."

Then he'd stick a finger in my gut and I would laugh along with everyone else because that's what you have to do sometimes. Baseball was a workout, but I was then as I am now, fat and stumpy. Thick, if you want to be polite about it. I always resented and picked at baseball's form-fitting uniforms. Thankfully, I could hide my rolls and pear head behind the padding and mask of catcher's equipment.

One year playing Select was enough for me. Sure, my knees started to feel pinched and panged but, more than that, I found that I didn't care about the game anymore. From the get-go, I'd never gotten much of a thrill out of baseball—I was always secretly terrified of being hit by a pitch—but I had a knack for it and had liked hearing my friends go on about how good I was. Maybe I was even a little better than good. But after my first year on Select, on the road and in locker rooms for the first time in my life, I came to understand that just because you're able to do something well doesn't mean that you absolutely have to do it. That's a lazy mistake that a lot of people spend their whole lives continually making.

Though I quit, Fitz didn't budge from his proud mound. He stayed on and, two springs later, at nineteen, he became the youngest player ever to open games for the Corbet Monarchs. The club is good to its players, pats their bums and scratches their backs. Managers don't like any of their guys thinking about anything outside of baseball and, since the Monarchs can't pay their players, they make it so no one has to work. Everyone gets a job within the organization. His first summer, Fitz worked as a groundskeeper who seldom kept any ground. Instead, he'd sneak me into the stad-ium at nights. We'd smoke-up in the dugouts and drink in the stands. He'd bring girls there to mash. His second summer with the club he toured Southern Ontario with former Monarchs' first baseman Derek Miller, helping him promote something called the Swing-O-Matic or the Perfect-O-Swing or something stupid like that. Basically, it was a contraption forged from ABS piping to help little-leaguers perfect their swings. Most mornings Fitz was so blurry-eyed, fuzzy-tongued and boozy-kneed that he couldn't manage to assemble the jumble.

For his third summer, the Monarchs employed him at their summer baseball camp, of all places. He coached kids, aged eight to twelve, of all people.

In his first year with the club, Corbet made it to the finals against Windsor. In a seven game series Fitz was responsible for clearing both benches five times. It was bad baseball, granted, but people love a rowdy good show more than they do fundamentals. As long as he lived, Jon Fitz would never throw a no-hitter, but he was a great showman. The papers nicknamed him the Maestro because he never gave a second thought to brushing back any batter with a little chin music, for whatever reason. If ever Fitz felt the game was getting too boring, or even if he was getting tired of it, he'd bean a guy. No hard feelings, that's just the way he rolled.

After years of yawning, I've come to understand baseball as, essentially, a communication sport, whereas most other sports can be understood as contact sports. In baseball, each team calmly ferrets out the solution to an argument through a kind of conversation, exchanging and communicating the ball all over the field. The resolution is soft and docile. For instance, if you strike out, you're simply wrong, but if you manage an inside-the-park home run you're right only because no one else could come up with a convincing rebuttal. One team ultimately makes a better argument than the others, and so the game is won. The sort of rough and tumble contact involved in a head-first slide into home plate pales in comparison to the sort of cathartic violence that you find in the average hockey or football game. But, though hardly acted upon, that gritted tension and aggression still exist in baseball.

Anyone who has ever played the game has surely considered how easy winning would be if you simply carried your bat with you once you've hit the ball. First base, second, on to third and all the way home, knocking out the teeth of anyone who got in your way. The tension is so taut that sometimes all it takes for the composure to snap is a hardball thrown intentionally at a batter's head. Jon Fitz speaks to this constant want of violence over boredom that everyone feels in the game, be they players or spectators. Players love a good brawl as much as the languid spectators do.

The sixth game of the Windsor series, Fitz threw at the head of Windsor's second baseman, Tim Wilkes. I don't know if it's true, but the story goes that he chucked that ball so fucking hard that it bounced off Wilkes' batting helmet, sailed above the stands behind home plate and landed in the parking lot. Fitz sets off car alarms. That was the first of two bench cleanings that game. His second movement of chin music had both teams piled-up and shoving on the pitcher's mound again. Fitz got beaten up pretty badly by Windsor. I'm sure he also took a few knocks of friendly fire from some of his own teammates, those few who resented his method of play. He opened the seventh game of the series with his left eyelid shining purple and swollen shut. Jon Fitz pitched his shittiest game ever, the Monarchs lost the series, but no one seemed to mind.

Frugh was on the lip of the jungle-gym's slide, rolling her weed into a tight little nugget. Unless you're into the sad and sagging breasts of the peelers by the highway or the unrefereed pell-mell of bar brawls downtown, Corbet offers little in the way of nightlife. Corbet's parks and playgrounds are, however, completely unpatrolled. She packed the tube, put her lips around the bottle and held the lighter to the repaired chamber. The water bubbled until she finally sucked the charred weed into the bottle. It bobbed, shrivelled black and buoyant on top of the water.

I could feel a mosquito feeding on the back of my leg. I let him eat for a second before I smacked and killed him.

Frugh held her smoke expertly, letting it escape slowly, the curlicues rising into the park's electric lights. The pot's musk overwhelmed the wet dog stink of the Gimlet.

"Yeah, that plastic's totally burning," she said. Her voice was tight as she passed the bottle to Fitz, who went through the same rigmarole. While he sucked up his smoke I poked in the gravel at my feet, looking for skipping stones and waiting my turn. Frugh was watching Fitz closely, smiling at his extra bit of eyebrow theatre as he sucked his own nugget through. He let the smoke creep out of his mouth and caught it with his nostrils. This guy.

Fitz passed the bottle to me as he picked himself up off the ground, walking over to the monkey bars behind us. Holding onto the highest bar, he dangled for a second. His feet lifted up underneath him, his knees half a foot above the sand, before he started effortless, mechanical chin-ups. He's like a kid that can't stand being still for any longer than it takes to get what he wants.

"So you work with kids too, huh?"

Frugh and Fitz were hitting it off. I popped and filled my lungs until they stung, tingling with the chemicals.

"Yup," he grunted, jutting his chin over the metal.

"Do you like it?"

" 'T's okay. Some of them really get my goat." Fitz is always laconic with women, letting them talk themselves out of things to say. He works under the haze of awkwardness like worm pickers work under a dim dawn. "You?"

"Yeah. I mean, you know, I like it okay enough. Most kids just scribble all over the page, or just draw the Simpsons and Spider-Man and stuff like that. But there's a few in my class that are, you know, pretty talented. Pretty talented for kids that young, right? I try to help those ones out. The other ones, the scribblers, are just glad to be left alone."

"Yep."

I could have resisted but I coughed out the smoke anyway, all sloppy, interrupting Frugh and Fitz's conversation and bringing the focus back to me. Frugh crouched by my side and slapped my back. The more I play-hacked the more I honestly needed to cough. I'd smoked an awful lot of pot last summer and my lungs sometimes got as weak and raw as when I began at thirteen.

"You don't usually cough."

"It's that tape," I wheezed, handing her the bottle, again feeling the grace of her attention.

"Matters never had much lung." Fitz dropped off the bar and sat back down next to Frugh, closer than he'd been before. "He always used to collapse during shuffle circles."

"I never collapsed."

"Right. You did."

I lied. Yes, I had collapsed once during our warm-up shuffles, but it had been a hot-as-balls day. Saying that I had never collapsed was more true than saying I collapsed all the time.

Frugh was rooting around in her zip-lock bag for more marijuana. "I would never have guessed that you played baseball, Matt."

"It's true. Most of my life."

"I'd love to see you in all that equipment sometime. Tight little pants. I bet it'd be a hoot." She lit her second popper.

"It's not a pretty sight," I said, having long gotten over my

33

physical awkwardness. It's always better to draw attention to your fat before someone else gets the chance to.

"Just because he was on the team doesn't mean he played," Fitz laughed. "He just sat there while I threw the ball at him. Like playing catch. And how many times did you get thrown out at first?"

"I was a better hitter than you were, Jon."

Frugh popped. "I thought pitchers never hit," she said, retentive, keeping her breath.

"Smart girl, this one," said Fitz, taking the bottle from her.

Shits and giggles. Oho! Shits and giggles at my expense went around our circle like the bottle as we popped a few more nuggets. I sat, saying nothing, while Frugh explained about her art class to Fitz who managed to act interested enough to keep her talking and aloof enough to keep her challenged. Same old. I thought less of Frugh, frankly, watching her dance this same ditzy dance I'd seen so many other girls immediately glean the steps to. I don't want to say it was hate that I felt, but maybe that's what it was after all.

She was supposed to have been different. Egyptian mother and Scottish father, Frugh McCulloch struck me as infinitely exotic, different than any other girl I had known. Not kowtowing to the same temptations and not informed by the same patterns of action and attraction. That one time we had kissed, I had tasted, in Frugh's mouth, an Egyptian spice and flavor that I couldn't place and had never tasted before.

But, then again, my knowledge of spices is limited.

According to some free weekly street rags, in the mid-'90s Corbet had been home to some of the better indie-rock bands in Canada. Only back then they called it *alternative*. But by the time Frugh showed up at the end of last year, the dredges of that original scene had relocated to Toronto and all that remained were a few hack high school kids murdering guitars and mumbling death lyrics in church basements. Frugh had missed the first boat but remained patient on the dock, hoping that another one would be by to pick her up. Who was I to tell her that that boat would never come, that

Corbet was now a dead lake?

When I met her that winter, Frugh was fresh from Oshawa and friendless. Idle, she was eager to hang out with just about anyone. She taught afternoon art classes to kids at the community centre where I still work as a custodian. Her shift ended half an hour before mine began and we started hanging out in that space in between, getting high—on my weed, by the way—out back by the dumpster. I was then and still remain a sucker for a woman wearing a man's oversized shirt backwards with the sleeves rolled up to the elbows. She always had paint splattered on her chest and dashed across her cheek.

Frugh was unlike the other women I'd known not only because of her heritage—which, in truth, had given her a nice cocktail of desert-sandy skin and pond-blue eyes—but also because she was excited about the idea of bumming around with me. Our dates began with us getting looped for that half-hour, four days every week. As winter ended she started stopping by my place after my shifts to smoke more pot and play Tetris on my old NES. In April we had tried jamming a few times, but neither of us could stand the tired idea of a guy and a girl harmonizing with two guitars and neither of us wanted to play bass.

The night we got so gone that we did our best to make out, she started laughing while my tongue was in her mouth. "My roof is ticklish," she had said. So that was that then. But we didn't need to have that sort of thing. At least, I didn't need to have that sort thing. Though I was attracted to her, the urge to see her naked gradually faded. That we were simply together, just me and her, was enough.

At first I revelled in introducing her to my few other friends because it was me that was presenting her to them, this beautiful creature that they all wanted so badly to make. She was a testament to my worldliness and ability to be friends with a knock-out girl without having to diddle her. She qualified and verified me. But when spring came in like a lion, when the dog shit from winter began to melt, Frugh began to seem bored. I had a hunch that she was my friend only because there had been no one else.

Phone calls started to come in, asking me what I was up to on Friday night, and if so-and-so would be there too. Less and less did I invite Frugh out with my other friends and she must not have known the right way to ask herself out without sounding desperate.

High, my skin grows more sensitive. Often I find myself, without realizing it, stroking my forehead or the slope of the bridge of my nose that bleeds into my cheek or the soft underside of my arm. It soothes me, a twofold satisfaction of the need to touch and the need to be touched. At times I coo, a cricket's pleasure. When I catch myself, a very lonely heat bothers my chest, a loneliness intensified by the high. Even lonelier is the feeling of being caught by someone else.

"What're you doing there, Matt?" Frugh opened the door of my inebriation and flicked the lights, letting little mean sniggers sneak in between her feet. I had been softly roaming the contours of my collar bone and clavicle, tracing the U at my neck and slipping my hand under the neck of my t-shirt, reaching as far as my shoulder.

"Nothing."

"He's feeling himself up."

"No!" Frugh was tickled. She even slapped her knee.

"I wasn't."

"You've never seen him do that before?"

"No. Never." She was becoming typical and she was becoming cruel but it was my fault for putting those two in the same place. She was supposed to be solid, immune, proving to me that Fitz's appeal was not absolute.

"That's nothing. This one time, when we were playing an away game in Goderich—"

"Jon. Don't. Okay?"

"What?"

"Aw, come on Matt. I want to hear."

"So we were staying the night over in Goderich at a Comfort Inn or whatever, right? And everyone on the team had to share beds.

Pitcher and catcher, me and Matters here had to share. In the middle of the night I wake up and …" Frugh started to chortle without having to actually hear the story "… and this guy here …" Ha, ha, ha, "… this guy here has got his arm around me, spooning, right? Stroking my hair and … and … he has this little erection—"

"No!" Frugh's in pieces and in disbelief.

"Yes! Yes! I swear to God. I wake up and he's holding me, feeling me up and he's got a boner jabbing me in the small of my back."

They laughed together like they were fucking. "Aw, Matt. That's so cute."

There was a pinch in my jaw, a firmness like a guitar string wound too tight. I was either going to cry or take a bite out of one of their arms. I couldn't decide which. Fitz is Fitz and will always be that way, but Frugh. Frugh was supposed to be better than all of that.

I took the stones I had gathered and got up to leave. Being high and sitting for so long, getting up and standing hit me fast. I couldn't help but lumber away slowly and cautiously, a lugubrious shadow disappearing into the bushes and down the river bank.

"Matt!" Frugh called from where she was sitting. "Come on! Don't take it so seriously. It's funny. That's all."

"He can be such a suck sometimes," I heard Fitz mutter.

"Yeah, well …"

I felt the weight of all the little stones in my palm. Bunched up in my loose fist I shook them, listening to them clink against each other. I kept shaking, gradually letting the gaps in my fingers widen, letting the smaller ones fall through until there were only three good big ones left. By myself, by the river, there is only ever loneliness and boredom, two indistinguishable waves of exhaustion. Getting my grip as right as I could, I tossed the first stone, losing sight of it as soon as it left my hand.

I only heard the splash.

The second good one I released too early and did little more than throw it at the water. The third one I kept a hold of, squeezing it and feeling it dent my palm.

***

I've got stories too, but I don't tell them. I have yarns that I could spin into such ugly sweaters.

I could have told Frugh about the time when, on an away game in Kingston, Fitz had had the shit beat out of him by a middle-aged woman. Me, him and the third baseman, Aaron Neilson, were drunk, loud and stumbling around downtown after winning our last game. At one point, Fitz wandered away from us and fell against the glass of a bank window. I didn't see her then, but there had been a homeless woman sleeping inside, or drinking inside, or doing who knows what in the bank, by the ATMs. What I also didn't see, though I was able to fill in the gaps just fine on my own, was Fitz's hand reaching into his pants, taking out his penis, and smooshing it up against the glass, doing his dance.

Laughing, Fitz joined us again, wobbling and putting away his junk, slapping our backs. The part of this debacle that I did see clearly, and can vouch for, was the bag lady—thinner than most, with tangled red hair, a sooty face and wearing navy flannel pyjamas—storming up soundlessly behind Fitz. Aaron and I could have drawn his attention to it, but both of us—me, at least—wanted to see how the situation was going to progress. The woman put him in a headlock which Fitz, giggling again, slipped out of easily. For him it was still a gas at that point. He was still fooling around. Without seeing her, he turned and came out swinging, knocking her in the jaw with everything he had. He realized who he had clocked and sobered up, blubbering apologies. But the woman was having none of it.

There must have been something wrong with her hands because her attack came from her feet at first. She kicked him in the stomach, the hip, the knees, the shin and the package that she had seen moments before pressed and distorted on the bank's front window. She was like a giant bird-woman, hopping up and down, screeching, her arms wobbling limp at her sides.

On the defensive, Fitz didn't hold back. He landed every punch, but that frail woman didn't register a single blow. He got her down on the ground at one point and slammed her head into the pavement. He did it again and still she was growling and snarling. By some grace of God, she had regained use of her hands and began to claw at Ftiz's face, peeling away large curls of his flesh. Aaron ran, but I stuck around to watch Fitz frantically fight for his life, to watch him yell, "Crazy bitch! Crazy bitch!" over and over again.

After a five-minute row the police arrived with their terse siren and broke up the wrestlers. It took two cops—a fat man with a moustache and tall woman with a ponytail—to tear the derelict from Fitz. Apparently the woman was a common character around the city, largely into vandalism and PCP. Like a boo-booed baby that doesn't cry until the accident and subsequent hurt is acknowledged by an adult, Fitz held onto his bawling until he was questioned by the cops. "I … I … I don't know what happened. We were just, we were just walking along—right Matt?—we were just walking along and out of nowhere that crazy bitch came up behind me and attacked me for nothing."

His chin was wrinkled, his cheeks red and gnarled, his snot a consistent stream carrying blood with it over his lips and onto the front of his shirt. It got to be so the fat cop had to hold him, patting his head and shushing promises that everything would be all right. Fitz deserved every bit of what he got served.

So, I could have told Frugh about that time or I could have told her about the time Fitz had his ass handed to him by an old man whose license plate he had stolen. The story unfolds in much the same way as the first: Fitz, drunk, does something stupid and is ripped apart by some sad and frail character. He weeps and ends up covered in the mess of his blood and tears.

Both times, when afterwards he asked me why I hadn't stepped in, I told him that I figured he could take care of himself. A character like Fitz is sustained only by constant success and will crumble to nothing upon his first loss.

The stories were there in my mouth, thick and vivid. I could've imitated Fitz's frightened yelps while Frugh rolled around in the sandbox nursing a busted gut. I could have brought it up, put on a dumb show of the stupid events, but I knew when I was beat. Fitz had already made me look petty and small and if I were to swipe back at him I would only shrink more.

If you can convince the other team that they've lost before the game's begun, then beating them is just a matter of keeping your arm fresh for nine innings. The thing with Fitz, though—why he's the worst baseball player I know—is that when you put everything you've got into every pitch you'll throw your arm dead by the fifth inning. At that point you're no good to anybody.

I sat on the damp grass and dirt and took off my shoes, dangling my bare feet into the Gimlet. The cool, thin water lapped at my ankles and tempered my hate until I gradually became loose and unravelled. Gently, I stroked the surface of the last stone I had yet to toss and felt the blood leave my face. In the silence I could hear a TV on in the houses on the other side.

Staying quiet at night in the residential streets of Corbet, you can to hear the chirp of televisions like that of insects you'd never notice unless you were listening for them. The murmur is a glum one because of the synchronicity: the same program is playing on every TV set, but is being watched separately, alone, inside each house, by people with nothing better to do on a Friday night.

Having tuned in myself, I didn't notice Frugh until she took a seat next to me. When I did notice her I went on pretending that I didn't.

"Matt?"

"Oh. Hey. What's going on?"

"Nothing. Are you okay?"

"Of course." I still wouldn't look at her. Another mosquito flew into my ear. I smacked the side of my head and killed it.

"Are you crying?"

"No."

"Oh."

"What?"

"Jon said that you were probably crying."

"I'm not. I'm fine."

"You're sure?"

"Yup. I was just really high. I needed to just be alone for a bit."

"You're good now?"

"Yeah. Oh yeah. No, I'm fine. You and Jon seem to get along fine."

Frugh undid her worn pink Chucks and submerged her own feet. She's the last person I'd ever guess to have a ring on her toe. It was small and amber and I thought it might have been a cultural thing that I didn't understand.

"That's terrible," she said finally. "What Jon did."

"It's okay. He makes fun of me all the time."

"No. I mean what he did to that kid."

"What kid?"

"You don't know?"

"No."

"You didn't know that he got fired from the camp? That he's probably off the team?"

I didn't know what Frugh was talking about, but it explained why Fitz had been drunk and hassling me at my home that afternoon. According to what he had told Frugh, which I suspected might have been a load, on the last day of camp the players and the campers play a game against each other. The counsellors are supposed to take it easy on the kids and let them win because the game's just for fun. One of the kids, an eleven-year-old brat who had been giving the other campers a hard time all week, called Fitz a "dirty rotten motherfucker" after Jon picked him off at first. On the kid's next at-bat everyone's favourite Maestro put all the mustard he had onto his fast ball and twinkled the troublemaker a few notes of his famous chin music.

"He said that all he wanted to do was to get the kid to duck and make him look like a pussy. Only the kid didn't duck. Broke his jaw. Police want to talk with him."

"Where is Jon?"

"He left. I don't know why you hang out with him. You don't seem to like him very much. He doesn't like you either."

"I don't hang out with him. He's just there sometimes."

It could have been true or it could have been bullshit Fitz had made up to impress Frugh further. Whatever. She came to me by the river more doleful than when I had left her, suddenly seeming very tired.

From her mother's side, so she says, Frugh gets hair on her arm, a thin black cover that she starts twisting when she's high. Everyone, when they're gone, has their own bit of business they'd rather keep to themselves but can't help but display. I find that most people are nose pickers. It's the risk you take when, in company, you smoke yourself into privacy.

We had nothing more to say to each other and not much else to do, so, in lieu of doing nothing, we kissed for a second time. Both our mouths were dry and we shared no sensations or tastes. Her finger grazed my temple, a long and soft tracing of what scant jaw line I have. I felt that more than I had anything in forever. I might have cooed, I don't remember. Frugh pulled away and with the light from the playground behind her I couldn't make out her face.

"Is there any pot left?" was all I could think to say.

"Enough for two poppers, maybe three."

"Do you want to finish it at my place?"

"Okay." Frugh sounded sad, but, then again, the human voice always sounds sad to me, like dog eyes which, when not overwhelmed by any great feeling, have a constant droop of melancholy and lethargy to them. We put our shoes back on and headed back. I slipped my one last stone, the best of the three, into my pocket. I'd try to cut the devil's throat some other time, when I had nothing better to do. Maybe when no one else was around.

Thirty-Six in the Cellar

ELI HAD ME at the end of my rope. He was making an unusually shrill fuss about getting into the car, triggering in me those blunt throbs of frustration and a fidgeting feeling in my fingers that whisper violence as a solution. A firm shake on the shoulder or a terse smack on his bum. Of course I would never lay an angry hand on my son, but when he's got me over a barrel, that feeling of desperation rises in my throat, and it makes me sick. I swallow and stuff that rage in the darkest most hidden basement of my guts.

Eli would not take off his Bob Pants costume. Or Square Bob Pants Sponge. Or whatever that goony character's name is. I can never keep all of his beloved cartoon creeps straight. Gert knows the guy's name. The get-up itself was little more than a bulky rectangle of holey yellow foam with glazed googly eyes and a stupid, face-wide grin through which Eli's own eyes peeked out. Forty dollars at the Spook Central in the mall, Eli would accept nothing but.

Gert would have had a fit. She would have taken him out of the costume kicking and screaming. For his own good, of course. But I didn't have the shins or the ears or the heart for it. For nearly that whole year, I had let Eli get away with murder: fights at school, shoot 'em-up cop shows after ten and candy for dinner. All for my own good, of course.

For all of October he wore that costume around the house. It was just me and that toothy invertebrate in chocolate-brown short pants. A strange cartoon stranger in place of my boy, there he would

43

be, at the dinner table sounding out the bi-syllabic words in his school readers or taking the trash to the side of the road or lazing on the floor in front of the TV watching DVDs of his coeval cavort and caper. Eli would only take his costume off to eat and bathe. At night, I had to wait until he fell asleep before I could gently extract him from it. Sometimes I'd forget that he was even a person in there.

That November 5th afternoon, I did my best to finagle my squirming seven-year-old into the front seat of our red VW Golf. Of course, there was enough space to swing a cat in the Windstar, but Gert had taken it. In the end, once we were already a half an hour late for Terry Sernaise's party, I had no other option but to lay Eli flat in the backseat, unbuckled. Gert would have had a conniption.

"I hate Mom," Eli had muttered once we were finally motoring. "I hate her, I hate her. I *hate* her."

This had been Eli's refrain since January. My forgetting to sign a permission slip for his class' fieldtrip to the Royal Ontario Museum had gotten the ball rolling. It was Mom's fault that he had to read quietly in the principal's office all day while his friends saw dinosaurs, not mine. My head hadn't been in the game; it had been up in clouds so thick and brooding that I just wasn't able to see Eli there beside me. A week after the ROM mix-up, I left him waiting two hours after his Beaver's meeting, standing on the stoop of the community centre with cold, red ears. Another time, I forgot him in the bathtub, where he went pruney and caught his death. All Mom's fault.

From February on, anytime something wasn't going tickety-boo in Eli's life—if his t-ball game was rained-out or if he didn't like the dinner I had burnt for him—he would slink back to his commiserative mantra. After nearly a year, his little bag of dynamite should have long been soaked harmless by overuse, but no. And even coming from a gawking, canary-yellow sponge, such seething, sure disdain remained a constant threat.

"Right." I said. "I know you do, kiddo."

"*You* don't hate her."

"Right," I said again, merging into the thin highway traffic.

"Well I hate her."

"That's not a nice thing to say about a person. Especially your mother."

"Well I *do*. And you should too." Still, Eli was getting mistaken for Gert on the telephone by telemarketers and old friends out of the loop. In his mother's voice he would say, She isn't home and I hate her and you should too.

"But I don't, buddy."

"But you should."

"Right. But I don't."

"You should."

"I don't, though."

"But you should hate her."

"Eli," I sighed, chewing skin from the insides of my cheeks, swallowing hard. "Come on, pal. Can we not do this now?"

By his silence I could tell that he was pouting. "Well *I* do," he huffed. I so wanted there to be one simple, tight bit of infallible wisdom I could impart to him—that he could soak up—that would make life suddenly clear and liveable. But all I had ever managed was a pathetic, That's not nice. Of course it's not nice. None of it is nice.

I looked to my right, hoping for some answers from my other passenger. With Eli squeezed into the back, I had had no choice but to prop my effigy next to me in the front seat, securing the belt across his shallow, leaf-filled chest. But he had nothing to contribute to our family spat. He only stared straight ahead with his permanent marker eyes, watching the auto malls, suburbs and traffic lights dwindle as we drove further into the sticks, towards Sernaise's farm. The snow clouds in the east were tinted a wan afternoon orange. My poor scarecrow had more morose issues weighing on his empty mind. For the four-hundredth time he would be tortured to death while our crowd looked on, singing.

What sad, sorry sacks we were, us three boys. All of us stuffed with kindling.

    With the car so thoroughly packed, there wouldn't have been room for Gert this year, anyway.

After all the fuss, we arrived just after four in the afternoon. The crescent moon was visible, waiting patiently for the sun to finish. Already there were fifteen or so cars parked on the Sernaise's front lawn, scattered pell-mell, leaving muddy, snaking tracks in the frosting ground. Judging from the cars, all the usual suspects were present again this year. The regular Guy Fawkes Day celebrants consist mostly of faculty members at Wyndham High and Sernaise family friends. But each year there is a friend of a friend that catches wind of this queer get-together and has to come and have a look for themselves. Some never come back and some come back with their own looky-loo friends the following year.

    Terry "So Crazy" Sernaise was born and spent the first nine years of his life in Summertown, just outside of Oxford. These days, at forty years young, any and all trace of a British accent is gone. The only remnant of his upbringing is an ardent observation of Guy Fawkes Day. Every November 5th he throws a party at his farm, far out on Rural Road 3. Friends and family get themselves up in costumes, eat BBQ, get a little lousy and finally burn an effigy of Guy Fawkes as soon as the sun goes down. So deep in the boonies, the bonfire can really roar, unencumbered. The flames snap like a murderer's footsteps in the woods, coming up behind you and gaining fast.

    Across the pond, costuming is not a nationally observed hitch of Guy Fawkes Day. It is, however, a small regional tradition that Sernaise upholds. Halloween was not celebrated in the town of his boyhood, but the late-October fun of dressing-up was gradually incorporated into the early-November Guy Fawkes hoopla. The Day has nothing to do with the Eve, make no mistake about it. The only connective tissue is that both parties dwell on those dark and dubious things that we otherwise choose to ignore. One day a year of lip service should be enough, I think. Who's hurt, then, if you're dressed as the Mummy or a Wolfman while you throw the make-believe carcass of Guy Fawkes into a snapping rager? Only the effigy.

The Sernaises occupy a modest acreage on the edge of Corbet. It has been in his wife Emma's family since the '30s. Since that time there have been few updates made on the three-storey farmhouse. Only the back deck is new, built by Terry a few years ago. The sinks, the cabinets, the wallpaper—all of it—still has the humble, dusty air of the Depression. Everything has the warm, worn feel of inhabitation.

A large red barn and a field where only long grass grows now is all that remains of a long gone agrarian age. The only animals the Sernaises keep are a gang of hoity-toity hens, one rooster, a mouser named Tim with a chip on his shoulder and two sheepdogs, Beany and Cecil.

Terry's is one of those plots that has slowed down the Urban Sprawl for years. Torontonian businessmen carrying briefcases filled with forms have been throwing oodles and oodles of cash at Terry since the '90s and still he refuses to sell. I say good for him. Let signs of the times be damned and leave our beloved boonies be.

Having found a space between a conifer-green Corolla and a babycrap-brown Oldsmobile, I eased Eli out of the back seat and was just as delicate getting Guy Fawkes from the front. I held him tight in my arms, his dry guts crinkling against my chest, and Eli carried our potluck contribution—Terry Sernaise's favourite apple pie—delicately out in front of him. We went around the back of the house to see if we could guess who was who.

This year's crowd was good. A little bigger than usual. Right away I identified Wyndham's principal, Maggie Johnson, who recycles her Pocahontas costume every year. It's a little inappropriate in its *Injun*ness, but we all know that her intentions are good. Of course, she noticed me, ever the clown. Next I saw Wyndham's math teacher, Keith Bruce—a mad scientist this year—who was talking to Mary Mathies, a murderous nurse, and her twelve-year-old son Dylan, a tattered hobo. Mary Szabo, the English teacher, was dressed as, I believe, Joan of Arc. The punk rocker I knew only by his first name, Adam. His wife's name—a Tina Turner—escaped me entirely. I placed the witch, the ghost, the vampire, the Vampira—a little chesty for a family event, as always—and the Jason. There was a gorilla in a business suit, not unlike the one I was wearing, that could have been anybody.

"Richard!" I turned around and it was Terry's wife, Emma Sernaise, standing on her back deck. She was dressed as the Man in the Yellow Hat, with a stuffed Curious George dangling from around her neck. By her side was her youngest daughter, Sara, also dressed as the Sponge.

When Emma clued in to the duplicate costumes, she let loose her lovely chortle, like the titter of Chip 'n' Dale in those old cartoons. Emma Sernaise is a roly-poly woman of Mennonite heritage whose apple cheeks are always flushed red with laughter. When she and Terry get going there's absolutely no stopping them. They will be in stitches on the floor and they never fail to bring the whole world down with them.

"Oh my. My, my," she giggled. "What have we here? How *will* we ever be able to tell the two of you apart?" Side by side Eli and Sara looked identical, Emma was right. I could only pick out Eli because of the pie in his hands.

"Emma. Hi. How are you?"

"Richie Rich. Oh, Richie Rich, I'm well. I'm well." Emma is also a bit of a louse, frankly. A wonderful and perpetually happy louse, though, that gets gaga with everything under the sun after just one fuzzy navel. "Bob," she said to Sara, "why don't you and *Bob* here go put the pie on the kitchen counter with the rest of the dishes?" The Bobs walked together through the sliding screen door and into the house.

"I like your costume, Emma."

"Thankya. Thankya," she gushed, stroking her chimp. "You're looking as clowny as ever, Richard. Clowny as ever."

I am always a clown, by the way. When I dress up, for whatever occasion, I am a clown. But I am always a clown and something else. I am a clown tennis player or a clown construction worker or

48

a beat cop clown. This year, for both Halloween and Guy Fawkes Day, I was simply a clown dressed as a regular man. From the neck down I was dressed as I would normally dress for my history classes: a smart grey wool suit from Moore's with a mustard-yellow dress shirt and maroon tie. From the neck up my face was painted white, my lips and ball-nose a bright red to match the tie. Up top I'm as bald as an underfunded school's basketballs, so my clowns always have Bozo hair. That is a naked pate with wild, fire engine red hair flanking the sides. Even though they kill, I put in contacts and painted little blue triangles above and below each one of my eyes.

What is funnier than a man that dresses up and pretends to be a clown? To my mind, a clown that dresses up and pretends to be a man is far, far funnier.

"And who do we have here?" Emma joked, leaning in and elbowing my doomed dummy in the side. "Mr. Fawkes I presume?"

"Indeed," I said, hoisting the effigy a little.

"Well, Mr. Fawkes," she said, shaking Guy's gardener's glove hand, "I suggest you enjoy the party while you can, because things will be getting pretty, pretty grim for you once the sun drops." She laughed like a raccoon in a tree. "Rich, why don't you and your friend go and find Terry? I'm sure that he's around here somewhere. Oh! Julia!"

Leaving Emma and her nosey chimp to greet a dinosaur, I waded into the crowd of pirates, Egyptians and aliens towards the curling smoke in the distance. The signals told me that Terry had started up the barbeque and was already burning the meat.

Sernaise is a small, squirrelly, middle-aged jester with a ten-year-old's buzz cut. He wears a kook's bushy black moustache and has a kook's crazy eyebrows. If you get him riled up enough he will literally pop his eyes out of his head and wobble them around. "The Bug Eyes," we in the faculty call it.

To his shop students, though, Terry Sernaise is known as "So Crazy" Sernaise. He commands a jovial respect and sees being thought of as crazy as a sign of this respect, as "major props." When he's working at his lathe or his jigsaw he sings to himself. He doesn't hum or whistle like any regular Tom, Dick or Harry. Terry Sernaise is a performer. Just the other day I caught him at his buzz saw singing a rousing round of "O, mares eat oats and does eat oats and little lambs eat ivy. A kid'll eat ivy too, wouldn't you?" Another time, I remember, it was "You give me fever when you kiss me. Fever when you hold me tight. Fevah!"

The only nickname my students ever gave me was the less than flattering "Dick-Bush" which, as Terry had once surmised, was "the male equivalent to the tuft of hair about the female pubis."

I'm not a hard or especially harsh teacher, but I'm no Terry Sernaise. When it's necessary I raise my voice and send students to the vice principal only as a last recourse. Even still, I'm the butt of many jokes around school. One is "What has two legs, two arms, a head, a leg, an arm, a head, two arms and two legs? Dick-Bush falling down the stairs."

It could be that I sing the national anthem over the morning announcements every morning or that I dress as a clown for every festive assembly's teacher's skit or that I trip on my own shoelaces more than most men my age. Or, my student's joshing could simply be a continuation of a lifelong trend of chain pulling. I have always been a hot mark for ribbing, my meekness and all. My mousy glasses, lanky body, bald head and the way I systematically agree to everything. Right, right, right.

The students call me names because I never nipped the problem in the bud. Because, with a shy smile and an eye roll, I let the name-calling go on. Really, it's my own fault.

This, funnily enough—or maybe not so funnily enough—was one of the five reasons cited on a list of complaints given to me by my now ex-wife shortly before she left our son and me last January. Secretly, I call them "bitch bullets".

Gert was a planner. She would go as far as buying my clothes for me and planning wardrobes for the weekdays and the weekend. She was also a list-maker. There would be Post-it Notes stuck all over the house with half-ideas and hurried instructions jotted down on them—grocery lists and to-do lists. She was always thinking, always worrying. It was no surprise to me, then, that in the months that she was preparing to leave me—leave *us*—I would occasionally find a brainstorming note with a few curious adjectives scribbled down, some crossed out and some underlined. In a way, when she handed in her final draft, I wasn't surprised.

Gert, in those months, had managed to whittle those countless adjectives, scattered all hodgepodge around our happy house, into a final top-five list. She typed her bitch bullets on WordPerfect and printed it out on our LaserJet printer. She had formatted the list so that it was perfectly centred in the page. The five words took up hardly any of the vast, empty white space of the paper. It looked something like this, only imagine a "polar bear in a snowstorm" sort of effect:

Richard, you are:
5. Too Nice
4. Too Boring
3. A Workaholic
2. An Introvert
1. A Pushover

When she submitted her five bitch bullets, neatly placed on a stack of marked grade nine papers on the War of 1812 first thing that Saturday morning, it had seemed so obviously silly. I wanted to crumple it up and toss it into the trash. Burn it maybe. Instead, I saved it. I tacked it on the cork board above my desk to laugh at. Only, that day I found myself coming back to it again and again, scrutinizing her five words and scrutinizing myself. The more time I spent with the list, the more apt it began to feel.

She approached me later that night. "So, I'm leaving," she had said.

"Right," I said.

Gert had reduced me to five intolerable adjectives, to my lowest common denominators. It was those five words, pinned into me like I was a bug on display, which allowed me to watch and do nothing while she hunted for a new apartment, divided our books, packed her clothes, took half the furniture, and drove off into the frozen streets. On her way out, the back tires of the Windstar slid and she crashed into a phone pole. Eli didn't want me to let her back in, but I did it anyway. I left her alone in the living room while she used our phone and waited for a tow.

Her leaving was not so different from the marriage itself. She did as she pleased and I complied. Right. I suppose that at one time she understood that compliance to be love. As did I. Maybe if, instead of saying Right, I had grabbed her hard by the arm and swung her around to me as she walked away, and if I had let her swing right into my fist, and if I had broken her beautiful Albertan nose, she would have stayed. If I had fallen on her and trashed the daylight out of her maybe, after it was over, she would have curled shivering into my arms and said she loved me and she was sorry. But I didn't. I only agreed with her that, yes, she was leaving me. Right.

Did she expect violence? If she had known me well enough to set out my clothes every morning, to even go as far as to buy all my clothes for me—if Gert had known me well enough to know that I would wear a wardrobe I hated because it was easier than saying I hated it—then she should have known goddamn well that I would have never said boo about her flight from us.

I have asked myself, every time Eli says he hates her, "Who's to blame?"

I didn't want our divorce to be so straightforward, where one parent is right and the other is wrong. All said and done, I wanted the end of our marriage and the end of our family to be as grey as snow clouds. Except a seven year old doesn't deal with greys so well. Eli demanded stark contrast. He wanted a villain and, maybe solely because he was living with me, he chose his mother. Dad was right and Mom was wrong. Right. Except Eli never saw the bitch bullets that Gert nailed to the cathedral door.

Before Gert left, Terry Sernaise and I had been only casual friends. We chatted at school, played the occasional game of basketball on weekends and, every year, I brought my full and seemingly functioning family to his farm to celebrate Guy Fawkes Day. Now we're thick as thieves. Every Sunday night, Eli and I drive to Sernaise's farmhouse and eat with his family, Emma, Haley and little Sara. I bring my famous homemade apple pie for desert. Like it was a death row last meal Terry Sernaise eats thirds with a two-scoop side of vanilla ice cream. Afterwards, he unbuttons the top button of his pants and let's gas escape from whatever end it pleases. The kook is a hound for good eats.

Having known So Crazy for nearly ten years, I know for a fact that Terry begins planning his costume no later than August. He has shown me some of the preliminary sketches. Only ever after the fact, though. Each year's new costume is a closely guarded secret, guarded with his life. Terry's a go big or go home kind of guy. In past years he has turned himself into a perfectly symmetrical half-man-half-woman, an easy chair, a Freudian Slip and the robot from *Lost In Space*. But this Guy Fawkes Day he had outdone himself.

As I had guessed, Terry was indeed by the barbeque, just a little to the left of the fire pit, which already had a modest flame wriggling. But the tongs weren't in Terry's hands. Instead, he was instructing his oldest daughter Haley—this year the moon—in his ancient art of overcooking a perfectly good hamburger patty.

"You want cross hatching," I heard him telling her. "Right angles. Ninety degree angles." His back was to me. Terry appeared as he always did, dressed in a red golf shirt tucked into tapered blue jeans, scuffed sneakers on his feet. Only he seemed much taller than usual. Gigantic. And he appeared to be holding something big and bulky in front of him. I approached slowly.

"What's the difference? No one sees it anyway," Haley whined.

"You can taste the difference."

"Dad. That's insane. You're insane, Dad."

I reached out and touched his shoulder. It felt unusually squishy. Fake. "Terry?"

He spun around and yelled out, "Richard! Help! I've been captured! He's gonna kill me!"

So Crazy Sernaise had gone and dressed as himself for Guy Fawkes Day. Sort of. He was Terry Sernaise being held captive inside of a wooden cage carried by a frothing mad Terry Sernaise, who was gripping a huge, rusty kitchen knife in his teeth. Somehow, in his wisdom and handiness, the real Terry—the captive Terry—had made a flawless double of himself. From what material, what red earth, what madness this twin had been forged, I couldn't say. But it was right on the money.

The mad Sernaise must have at least been a little bit kind. He had allowed Terry one last beer in the cage before murdering him.

"Terry!"

"Ahhh!" He clutched and shook the bars of his cage, gritting his teeth and rolling his Bug Eyes manically before he cracked up and let out his wheezing, dusty laugh.

It took me a minute to understand the schematics of Terry's illusion. From the waist up, his double was fake, but the murderer's legs belonged to the actual Terry. In the cage, from the waist up, Terry was the real deal, but the captive Terry's legs, crossed beneath him, were props. The cage covered up the seam. A sight to behold.

"You're looking sharp there, Rich. Tried, tested and true, Bozo. You know, there's a gorilla dressed as a businessman that you really should talk to."

"Right. I saw that. Yeah."

"She's an old friend, very nice. You'll want to flip those, Haley. No, with the spatula, not the tongs." From his cage, Terry looked out over his backyard, busy and colourful with festooned adults laughing and drinking, loving the chilly and bright afternoon sun. He breathed a mellow sigh. The autumnal air smelled of burnt pine. "So, you brought Fawkes."

"I did."

"Looking good. Looking good. Doppelganger, right? What did I tell you?"

"It *is* strange, huh?"

Terry pointed his beer to a weathered Adirondack chair by the fire pit. "Why don't you go put that treasonous old Catholic by the bonfire?" Terry took a swig, and made a satisfied "ahhh" as if he were in a commercial. "And get yourself a beer while you're at it. The chow'll be ready in no time. You'll want to turn those, Haley. No, no. Counterclockwise. Counter. Counter."

Each year I devote one of my grade twelve classes to Guy Fawkes Day. For my students, this means a free period where they don't have to take notes, even though I encourage it. This is the gist:

Queen Elizabeth I was a booster of the Protestants and a bully to the Catholics. So, when the old girl kicked the bucket in 1603, the well-meaning, oppressed Catholics had their fingers crossed that her successor, James I, would be more affable. No such luck. James proved to be as tried and true a bully as old Liz and, under his thumb, the Catholics got ever sorer.

In fact, they became so sore that thirteen of them packed the cellar beneath the House of Lords with thirty-six barrels of gunpowder. That's an awful lot of gunpowder for one Protestant. The assassination plot was foiled when one or more of the thirteen men got squirmy with qualms and blew the whistle, snitching on their co-conspirators. A man named Guy Fawkes (known as Guido in some circles) was discovered in the basement with his thirty-six barrels on November 4, 1605. He was tortured throughout the night and eventually had his bucket kicked for him on the 5th.

The twelve stragglers were eventually rounded-up and you can be sure that they dangled from their necks at the gallows.

Understand, that group of thirteen, of which Guy Fawkes became a poster-boy of sorts, were only standing up for themselves. They were pushing against an antagonistic force. They were right to want to fight back.

But thirty-six barrels of gunpowder! That would have been one humdinger of a blast! Their plan was to assassinate James I, but an explosion thirty-six barrels large would have taken out a whole lot more than one man. It would have crippled the Parliament and either killed or injured everyone inside. There would have been a slew of bystanders that would have kicked it right alongside the man who the plotters gripe was honestly with. This, some say, is why the whistle was blown. And a good thing it was, too.

The gang was so concentrated on the assassination of one man, overtaken by a monomaniacal devotion to their plot, that all those innocents became blurred and faceless in their periphery. That's abominable. That's not justifiable. And that's the sort of tunnel vision that makes history history. The many are forgotten and the few are remembered.

So, what is being celebrated, then, when Guy Fawkes, in one form or another, gets tortured annually for exactly four hundred years?

Guy Fawkes was as British as the civilians he would have killed with his blast. That's why it's treason. It wasn't a foreign attack. It was an inside job, the worst. To add to this, the warring factions were both Christian, two groups who had a slightly different view. But those slight differences were enough. Christians were oppressing Christians, and Brits were planning an attack on Brits.

What is being celebrated, as near as I can tell, is the sussing-out and removal of the diseased parts of a whole. The process isn't nice and it isn't black and white. It is necessary. To kill a man that commits treason is to saw off a gangrenous limb in order to salvage the whole body. Keep fair and unfair out of it. The body must live, either with two legs, or one leg, or no legs. For better or for worse, a sacrifice needs to be made.

Following a delicious round of medium-rare weenies and burgers, Terry got tipsy and overbearing enough to take the tongs away from his dear satellite. After a second, over-done helping of gristly charred meat, everyone had had about their fill of the grill. By that time the western sky was lousy with gunmetal clouds showing their grape-fruit underbellies. Everyone's attention was focused on the looming punishment. Us regular celebrants were atwitter with what we knew the darkness would bring and the newbies were atwitter with anticipation of finding out. That year I fell somewhere in between. All the old felt oddly new.

That Guy Fawkes Day was the first time out mingling in public since the split. Gert had always walked me through parties, and I had willingly followed her, gracious for her making the yammering customs of soirée's easy on me. To lubricate myself tonight I had a few more beers than usual. Everyone wanted to talk with me about the divorce. "How was I holding up?" Just fine and dandy, thanks. "Did I know it was coming?" I could feel that things were not as they should be, but no, I didn't think it would ever get to that point. "And the future?" What a silly question to ask a high school history teacher. While there are discernable patterns in history, the sea changes are what really make and break the world.

"The future's not ours to see," was the best I could come up with.

"Well, we feel for you. What a terrible thing for a mother to do."

"Right," I said. A terrible thing for a mother to do, indeed. To leave her boy behind like that. Gert never explained why, exactly, but really there could be only two reasons. Either it was a gesture of selfishness or one of compassion. Unless it was that she wanted a fresh start, then she had to have thought I needed Eli more than she did. That's both a terrible thing for a mother to do and a terribly hard thing for a mother to do.

All afternoon, I did my best to smile, to be kind. I had to try harder than I had ever tried to stifle the urge to tell these kind people to piss right off, to keep their noses out of my own sensitive, privileged business. But I joked and laughed the gravity away. While I was being drilled by well-meaning colleagues, friends and friends of friends, I noticed the handsomely dressed gorilla hovering like someone who had found a sack of cash on the street but was nervous about being seen picking it up.

I was on the deck getting myself a fresh beer when the beast finally pounced. In the field, the children were chasing each other and Beany and Cecil were chasing the chickens. I couldn't recall the last time I had seen Eli.

"Do you get it?" the voice asked, muted and nearly inaudible from inside.

"Sorry?" I looked up.

The gorilla removed its fangy mug. Inside was a sweaty, vexed middle-aged redhead. Her face was dappled by freckles and she had blackboard-green eyes. It must have been stinking hot in that head. She looked about ready to drop. "My costume," she said. "It's a joke. Do you get it?"

"Right. Your costume." I looked over my shoulder. Sernaise was chatting with a Tin Man and a Batman but still managed to observe the two of us from his cage, out of the corner of his eye.

"I'm a monkey in a monkey suit. Get it? A monkey in monkey suit."

"Right. Of course. And I'm a clown dressed as a guy."

She laughed. "I can see that." We were both laughing, though I didn't and she couldn't have found anything funny about anything. "I'm, uh. My name's Mary." I shook her big mitt. Her rubber ape fingers were long and floppy and they patted the inside of my arm. This chance meeting stunk of a scheme. I knew it, and I didn't like it.

"Mary. I'm Richard. Dick, actually. Dick Bush."

"Dick Bush?"

"That's right." I took a sip and lingered with my beer.

"Good to meet you."

"Good to meet you, too. You're a friend of —"

"Emma's. Originally. I've known the two of them for years."

"Nice people."

"Great people."

"Good family."

"They are."

"Hm."

We smiled affably and drank our beers. I finished mine and grabbed at another. I was trying not to be cross with Mary, but a sour taste kept biting the sides of my tongue. From out of nowhere, a squealing Spider-Man and a winded princess ran between us. Spidey took cover behind Mary and the princess stalked him from behind my back. Mary and I froze and exchanged wide eyes, pretending that we weren't there or that we were trees, maybe. The princess had hold of my arms, clutching them, ready to dart out in pursuit of the web slinger as soon as he made a move.

An urge struck me to turn and hold the princess while yelling, "Run, Spider-Man. Run!"

But he didn't need my help. Spidey stepped left, fooling the princess, and then shot off right. The little girl nearly threw me to the ground pushing off after him. Mary and I laughed and laughed and laughed and laughed. Oh, we laughed. As long as we kept making noise everything would be peachy.

If only Eli would come to me in tears with a scraped knee. I had no idea where he was, but I wanted him and I needed him. Again, he'd slipped my mind completely. I hadn't seen him since I sent him into the house with Sara, the other Sponge.

Right away, I had sniffed out Mary to be a recent divorcee, full of brooding and nagging pangs of inadequacy just like poor old me. We see each other like I imagine only ghosts can really see other ghosts. I supposed the two of us could sit down and have long, commiserative, cathartic conversations about the decision, the procedures and the difficulties of raising children on our own. But that was only sad shoptalk and I didn't want any of it.

With a mouse in his teeth, Tim the cat trotted proudly past us and laid it on the top step of the sliding glass door. I began to glance over Mary's shoulder, to see if I could spot my son. In the distance, I saw a Sponge, but couldn't be sure if it was Eli or Sara.

"You know, Mary ..."

"Yes, Dick?" she said, smiling and cocking her head to the side, maybe trying to rein in my wandering eyes.

"A gorilla's an ape," I said.

"Sorry?"

"You're in a gorilla costume and a gorilla's not a monkey. It's an ape, like I said. A great ape I think. So, technically, your costume is an ape in a monkey suit."

"Is that right?"

"Technically, yes. But it's still a great costume. An ape dressed as a monkey. That's still really funny. Really."

"Right. This was all the costume shop had." Mary held up the gorilla head in her long hands, offering it as an excuse. What an asshole thing to say. For what might have been the first time in my life, with my back against the wall, I had been a fuck, a shit, a bastard. Mary was no good at this and I was even worse. We were dizzy and clumsy like leaving a theatre after sitting through a long movie. Our legs would come back in time, okay, but pins and needles can't be rushed.

"I see. Will you excuse me, but I have to go and find my son. Make sure he's doing okay. The other kids pick on him."

"Sure. Of course. It was nice to meet you, Dick."

"Nice to meet you too, Mary."

I did my best not to scurry away, not to flee like I had just stuck up a liquor store. This wasn't fair. Asshole. I should have kept up the conversation until Mary felt awkward enough to walk away and leave me standing by the cooler alone. That was the very least I could do. Beelining towards the Sponge I hoped was Eli, I saw and did my best to avoid that sneaky matchmaker, Terry. But he managed, with some difficulty, to catch up to me.

"Mary's a sweetie, eh? You guys seemed to hit it off. What do you say?"

Right then, I forgot all about Eli. I was compelled suddenly to clean Terry's clock, to punch out his lights. But I managed to stifle that impulse by focusing my rancour on something else. "I say that the sun's nearly gone down all the way. It's high time we put Guy into the fire."

The effigy duty rotates annually. Last year Susan Barnes, a friend of Emma Sernaise's, brought the effigy. The year before that it was the math teacher Keith Bruce. He went out of his way, I remember. He did his homework, looked at some engravings on the internet, and showed up with a historically accurate effigy of Guy Fawkes, from the tips of his buckled boots to his curly mop. Traditionally, though, the body is only supposed to be made of old clothes that you have lying around the house, stuffed with leaves.

So Crazy Sernaise had come into the history office on the first day of October still wearing his safety goggles and his apron covered in the motes of his shop room. "Rich," he said frankly to me like he was offering a diagnosis, "this year's your year."

"For the effigy?"

"Right. I think it would be good for you, seeing a scarecrow made out of your old digs burn on a pyre."

"I don't know if I'll be coming this year, Terry."

"You're in charge of Fawkes. So you have to come. That's that. Good. So, I better get back to class and make sure no one's lost a finger." He removed his thumb like a parlour magician and left.

Keeping with tradition, I had constructed my Guy Fawkes out of my old, unwanted clothes. Eli and I had dressed him in a pair of "smart" chocolate slacks from the Bay and a "very current" sky blue V-neck sweater, under which was a "sharp and complementary" eggshell shirt, both from Mark's Work Wearhouse. On his feet was a "sensible and comfortable" pair of loafers from Payless, only ever worn twice. Aside from the head, which was a papier-mâché cast of a balloon that Eli had painted features on, Guy Fawkes was, this year, the spitting image of the me that I had been on Saturday afternoons passed; the me that Gert had carefully picked out for me.

Murderers' feet were in the air and embers flitted above us and died out like fireflies. Dusk was giving into the night and as the bonfire grew, shivering more violently, it drew the revellers in. It happens naturally, no one needs to be herded. The burning of the effigy is the main attraction. But all the kids were still off hiding and being sought after. I wanted to cup my hands to my mouth and call "Ollie-ollie-oxen-free" over the field and into all the nooks and crannies where they were hunched and quiet. Eli should be here to see this, I thought. He loved this part. Every seven-year-old boy loves anything burning.

Sernaise came up to my side, my Saturday-afternoon-Guy-Fawkes slung over his shoulder. Empties rattled around in his cage. He was lit, as he always was on Guy Fawkes Day. Myself, I was a little further into the bag than I should have been. In the past, Gert had remained sober, so this year I had to try and be the responsible one.

"Well, Rich, what do you say? Do you want to do the honours?"

"Yes," I said, snatching my body from him. Then, suddenly unsure. "What do I do?"

"Just toss him on."

All eyes were on the clown pretending to be a man. The heat from the blaze was welcome. The reasonable weather had called it quits as soon as the sun went down and everyone was blowing warm air into their hands. Mary, who I assumed had left early, would have been snug as a bug inside of her ape. As I got closer to the fire's perimeter the smoke stung my eyes, already stinging with contacts, and I could feel my clown make-up beginning to harden and crack, tugging at my skin, open up fissures revealing my flesh beneath. There was a man beneath the clown incognito as a guy and he was peeking through the chinks.

I looked back at Terry. His Bug Eyes were full of flames. He nodded his head and made a little tossing motion. It looked like he was doing a hula dance, sitting down in his cage.

It has happened for four hundred years and it will probably happen for four hundred more. Guy Fawkes went into the fire. All of us Canadians applauded the burning of England's wonky leg. We may walk on crutches but, goddamn it, we will walk. We might never run again but we will hop and take wider steps than ever before.

I returned from the fire and took a seat in the Adirondack where Guy had been and watched my effigy curl and snap in the flames. I wanted him dead and I wanted him to feel each and every inch of his encroaching death by fire.

Terry led those who knew the words in song: "Remember, remember, the fifth of November, gunpowder, treason and plot." As if filled with little fires, smoke rose from all of our singing mouths and into the cold night. "We see no reason why the gunpowder treason should ever be forgot."

Guy Fawkes' face was the first part to disappear entirely into the flames. It burned quick, maybe because of the chemicals in the papier-mâché's glue. Then the rest went wavy in the heat, becoming black and slowly disappearing. Up I went. Ten years of Saturday afternoons turned to ash. Everyone sang and celebrated and I mouthed along with the words. I was sure that we were all murdering him for our own reasons.

The sacrificial smoke writhed and twisted in massive curlicues. We sang and we sang, promising never to forget. You can take the plotter out of the basement but the powder kegs will always linger as a reminder, still gathered there under the House of Lords. We're all responsible and we promise and promise and promise not to forget about those un-ignited barrels.

Feeling someone come up beside me, I turned from the bonfire to find Bob Pants. He had come from out of the woods, from out of nowhere to stand next to my chair and watch the sacrifice. In the glassy, plastic whites of his ersatz eyes, the fire was especially clear.

"Bob Pants," I said. "I do hate your mother. I hate her so much."

He looked at me through his teeth quizzically and then turned back to the fire. I was thinking of something more to say, searching again for that exact maxim that would sum it all up and set him on a straight and narrow path. Before I had a chance, he was shoved from behind by a runt George W. Bush.

"It!" the President shouted.

"Hey!" I shouted back. That push was too much, too hard. Bob fell forward a little, but got up on his own and chased W in circles around me. I tried to grab at the President, but the two of them scooted away before I could get a grip. Off they went into the dark parts of the field that the bonfire didn't light.

An hour later I found Eli, tuckered out and sleeping on the Sernaise's couch, out of his costume. We, Gert and I, used to stand in his doorway at night and watch him sleep, watch him twitch and quiver while he dreamt. The desire to pet him a little would always warm me and clutch hard inside my chest. Gert would tell me not to do it, so I would wait until she fell asleep before getting out of bed and going back to his room. It was one of the few times that I would defy her. Eli sleeps so silent, I worry that alarms and sirens will go off if I so much as touch him. But I always have to graze his cheek with my thumb or pat his hair, just to be sure that he is really real.

It was late, way past his bedtime. Way past mine. Eli woke a little when I lifted him out of the cushions and into my arms. "Pizza Day form," he muttered.

Carrying him to the car, I ran into Terry Sernaise who was directing the traffic on his front lawn. Heavens be praised, he had gotten out of his cage and escaped his murderous half. Good for him.

"Thanks for having us over again, Terry. It was a great time. Really great."

"Wouldn't be Guy Fawkes day without you."

"Well, we're off." I patted Eli on his tush. "I've got to put this kid of mine to bed. But we'll see you tomorrow night, huh?"

"Tomorrow night. Don't forget that pie."

"I won't."

"Take care."

"You too."

"Wait. Terry?"

"Yep?"

"The thought was nice but I never want to have to meet another fucking gorilla, okay?"

"Right," he said.

I balanced Eli on my shoulder in order to free up a hand to shake with. Terry Sernaise's a good guy. I like him a lot. He can be a little overbearing, though. With that same free hand I fumbled with my car keys, trying not to drop my son. Unconsciously repeating Pizza Day form to myself, I realized what Eli had been murmuring about. I had forgotten to fill out the form for his class's Pizza Day next Friday. I made a note to make a note about it when we got back home.

I fit Eli into the passenger seat and buckled him in tight. Pizza

Day form, I said, over and over again in my head, heading home. The highway lights washed over Eli, sending him into darkness before illuminating him again, only to claim him again. Don't forget. Two slices of pepperoni, a chocolate milk and a fudgesicle.

The next night things were oddly tense between Terry and me, though he did his best to mask it by being overly jovial at dinner. After pie was gobbled and pants loosened, Terry, serious like I had never seen him, grabbed me tightly by the arm and pulled me aside. "Listen Rich," he said, "what's the big idea, huh?" His Bug Eyes bugged out at me with ire instead of the usual twinkle. He looked about ready to throw down.

"What? Terry, what's wrong?"

"What's this, huh? About you telling my little girl that you hate her mother?"

Old Hardy Boys

JUST TO THE SIDE of the apartment building's stoop were erected some display tables and a few racks of clothing. And a sign that said "Moving Sale." Cathy was handing over a Harry Belafonte double album—"Live from Carnegie Hall"—to a young girl dressed like a little old lady save for the sneakers.

"Isn't that mine?" I asked.

Cathy took the album back from Grandma Style and stared hard at it, felt it in her hands, as if its shape and weight might evince the ownership. "Is it? I don't know. Do you want it? A buck."

"Um …" Grandma Style started.

"No. Forget it. She can have it."

Holding the record under her arm the girl browsed the tables and fingered the racks again quickly before leaving for good. There were a few other students and junk collectors, mulling. Maybe Cathy had lost weight or cut her hair since I had seen her last, God knows how many years ago now. She was always doing that, though, cutting her hair and losing weight, growing her hair or gaining weight. "You took all your stuff."

"Well. I don't know. Maybe I missed some things. Some of this looks familiar."

"So go ahead and take a look around I guess. Let me know if you find anything you think's yours and we'll haggle."

"I didn't know you were moving."

"Why would you?"

Cathy raided second-hand stores compulsively, absolutely

gutted them. That any item was cheap, old and tacky was enough to make her want to absolutely have it. The clothes racks dipped under the weight of gaudy outfits—skirts, dresses and men's tuxedos of puce, mauve, and periwinkle—that she had once absolutely *had* to have. There were stacks and boxes full of old *National Geographic*, *Popular Mechanics* and *Life* that she'd scooped up with the intention of making collages and art projects, though she never got around to doing it.

Other men flipped through her books, curiously. I supposed that they might be rooting around in Cathy's junk trying to find something they had forgotten themselves. Everything on those tables looked familiar to me, but I'm sure that some of it Cathy bought long after we'd been together. It was difficult for me to tell whether I'd owned something or was just used to seeing it around. To be sure, I opened the front covers of some books to check for my initials.

Behind a table full of busted television sets—for a diorama project she had been planning just when we had started going out—was a boy, about five, sitting with his legs up and crossed on a wooden chair painted pink. His head was turned down into an old *Hardy Boys* book, which Cathy had once picked up to give to her father on his birthday.

I leaned over the TV's and whispered at him, "Hey, kid." His head jerked up and he looked at me, startled. At what point in your life do you stop responding to "Hey, kid?" I wonder. His face was wide and flushed red in the brisk afternoon air. By the day's standards, he was dressed hip, blue jeans rolled at the cuff and a flannel farm boy's jacket, flipped at the collar. Smack dab in the middle of his forehead there was a price tag. $3. He licked at a tear of snot that had wept onto his lip.

"Forget it," I said, strolling away slowly with my hands in my jacket, without saying goodbye or good luck or anything.

Pardon Our Monsters

ONTARIO'S SPRINGS SMELL of shit and rot. Bodies of road kill and strays that froze in the winter turn muddy and ripe in the season's turnover. Tiny pagodas of feces thaw and reek anew. We were hiking through this muck, through the living dead mess, to our fort to get up to what we usually got up to. Out of everyone's way, we thought our spot was über secret. That was a word we used to death: über this and über that. The summer before, we had built the fort in the sparse woods between the old farmer's field and the Galt Cemetery by Highway 6, where the Wal-Mart is now. Our first time out since the fall, we had to foot it. My bike had been stolen two months before and Joshua's a week before that.

The day was overcast. After a week of summer preview, the sky had opened up with piss again, uncovering and revivifying. In this seasonal waft of organic stink I picked up on an uncommon, synthetic shade. And eventually, against the grey clouds, another more earthly plume made itself known.

Dennis Miner had been dead two months by then, by the end of May.

Me and Josh would light out to our hideout, where we'd look at the porno, smoke the cigarettes, and drink the beer we filched from Joshua's older brother Geoff. While serving in the Gulf he'd been shot in the spine by friendly fire, so stealing from Geoff was easy. Joshua himself never looked at the magazines much. Mostly he watched me from the opposite corner as I ogled the open women, my hand fidgeting around inside of my jeans.

No doubt it would have been a lovely masturbatory afternoon of damp palms in late spring had not the fort been on fire.

To see our boys' club burn was an über terrible thing. Right then was the spring of our discontent, call it.

We had built the sturdy base first and then erected plywood walls where we eventually tacked centrefolds and pictures of electric guitars. Using a dusty green tarp, we did up a roof so we could jerk-off in speckled emerald penumbras as the rain fell all around us. We would think about how we wouldn't have to jerk off if we had guitars and knew how to play them, because centrefolds would just fuck us if we knew how to double tap a cherry Strat. Double tap without looking. Not looking was key. We understood that as one of life's fundamental truths. At least this is what I thought about. I can't speak for Joshua.

Miraculously, the teetering eyesore, resting like a bird's nest in the crotch of an old oak tree, had survived that first frigid Ontario winter. Having proved its mettle, there it was anyway, our lovely secret rendered biblical—sizzling and crackling, red and black, undulating like waves. The tarp sent out a repugnant stench. Even overpowering the stinks of spring, like action figures burnt in backyard rituals. Our fort might have survived the cold winter, but even colder were the hearts of a murdered saint's asshole brothers.

Smut in hand, an emptied Coke jug of boozy cocktail in our knapsacks, we stood agog. The fire was unbelievably real-looking. So real it was surreal. We gathered up our slack jaws when the first rock fell at our feet, spraying our jeans with mud. We looked up and there were Shane and Wayne Miner, hiding in the bramble surrounding the other side of the clearing. They were laughing at us with their typical Miner rictus.

"Fuck off queer fags!" they shouted. A second rock landed behind us. It had come from Wayne, for whom everyone was either a queer, a gay, a fag, or any combination of the three. Wayne was the one, though, who would sneak up behind you in the hall at school, grab your hand and put it on his unwrapped, hard pecker. "Hey buddy," he would whisper behind you, in a raspy, sultry way, just as you felt him poke your bum. "Hey. Hey buddy, mind if I bum a fag?"

The third rock came from Shane and hit Joshua on the left side of his head.

Joshua fell behind me like a sack of potatoes, nudging my shoulder as he went down. He was sprawled, prostrate in the tall grass, amidst a few scattered beer bottles, cigarette butts, and condom wrappers. The left side of his soft face was covered in glutinous black blood and seasonal muck. There were only grubby chortles from the other side of the flames. The Miners took off running and jumped the tall fence of the cemetery.

Wayne made it over fine, but the elastic cuffs of Shane's track pants snagged on the fence's metal twist. Banging the front of his body on the links, he fell forward. Shane dangled there, confused and terrified, a discombobulated pout on his wine-stained face. A look like he was the victim, fleeing for his life. For that one moment everything was a gas: base of operations ablaze, best friend lying dead at my L.A. Gears, retard Miner brother dangling from the fence like a fish on a hook.

Shane wriggled out of his pants like he was being shat out, until he was in an L-shape on the ground, fighting to get his feet loose. In his navy briefs, his scrawny legs a milky white, Shane stood on tiptoe and finagled his pants from off the twist. Slinging his trackers over his shoulder, he took off into the cemetery, chasing after his long gone brother, disappearing behind the rows of tombstones.

Bastards, always hiding behind graves.

An ugly fucking gang, there were initially three Miner brothers. There are now just the two. All three were as dumb as a wet sack of hammers and each was equally obsessed with lighting trash cans, especially those either directly behind or in the near vicinity of fast food restaurants, on fire. The greasy contents of wrappers and cardboard burger boxes lent itself nicely to both a beautiful and long burning pyre. Their blazes were so personalized that, when you passed by them, you knew exactly who had dropped the match with such careless tender loving care.

Blame violence, recklessness and sass mouth on poverty. Go ahead. Blame pyromania on hand-me-down clothes and unpaid cable bills; on fathers who weren't there in one way and mothers who weren't there in others; on a diet of microwavables and an income consisting entirely of scratch-and-win jackpots. Go ahead, I fucking dare you. To cast such silly aspersions is to flout that ignoble fact that, yes, some people are straight-up motherfuckers regardless of their rearing and station.

Besides, the Miner family occupied two houses, side by side, and no family with two houses could possibly be as mendicant as you think their destructive nature might suggest.

The youngest was Shane, who had a purple wine stain on his right cheek. His hair was so blonde it was white and he had blue eyes that were washed out like blind dogs I have seen. Shane was my age, was in my grade, and so was my personal tormentor. In our grade six class, for a lark I guess, he once tried to stab our teacher, Mr. Stephenson, in his big fat belly with a blue ball point pen. Shane jabbed so quick and thoughtlessly that he missed the meat and hit his belt instead, exploding the ballpoint. There was blue all over Stephenson's fine white shirt like there was burgundy all over fuckface's piebald mug.

Wayne was the oldest brother, who was my sister Diane's age. His dick was always out, waggling, held between thumb and fore like he was a Marine Land trainer using dead fish to bribe tricks out of a dolphin. One afternoon, according to a yarn Diane often spins, Wayne Miner started whacking-off beneath his desk.

The time was last period, the class was eighth-grade math and the cast of students began to notice the dull sound of a fist thumping on wood. It was a knocking like a class cutup's ruse to fool a teacher into thinking someone's at the door. By the time the duped teacher had peeked into the hallway the class had identified the source of the commotion.

With a shit-eating smile on his face and his puny cock pumping in his fist, Wayne stood up like he was about to accept a major award. Drawing a straight, white viscous line into the sandy beige of the chic knapsack, Wayne came all over Diane's bag.

The teacher—whatever her name was, young and pleasant, new and always labouring to be completely chill with what went on in her classroom—accepted Wayne's challenge. She crossed that cum line with savage gusto.

Good for her.

These brothers, these fucking brothers, were fantastic archaeologists, deftly plumbing the annals and ugly cores that were long lost and ignored in so many people. Diane tells me that her teacher was so amazed, flushed and flummoxed, that, with a flat open palm, she belted Wayne square across the chops.

That young woman probably felt, after that first smack—her hand buzzing—that she had it in her to kill a boy. That boy. That Wayne Miner boy. And no doubt it terrified her. In her quiet life, murder was suddenly a glorious and justified option. She felt she could beat him to death with all the bones in her body, her bones knocking against his until one or the other turned to dust and fluid marrow. Because she kept at him, swinging her palm and the back of her ringed hand with greater and greater fervour, crying.

It's anyone's guess why she cried, dread or joy. Or maybe it was only the steam released when the valves of all that is cruel and animal in every human belly is opened and comes whistling out.

She beat Wayne and he took it. Those dirtbag brothers always took it. They instigated but would not defend themselves. This way, in the end, after they had been pummeled, the person who was initially abused becomes the abuser and the Miners the victims. Wayne got a week off school and that teacher got fired. My guess is that she probably never taught again.

Come unprovoked stabbings or high, cresting waves of spunk, after what happened to their brother, you couldn't touch these two incorrigible hoods.

Dennis was the middle Miner brother, one year older than me, so not too old to boot fuck me if ever he felt taken by the fancy. At the end of March, his grade seven year, he was mowed down by a yellow Geo. The accident happened right in front of his house. The Miners lived not far from our school, where Dennis would have been sleeping safely at his desk had he not been wasted and ditching class.

The accident wasn't the driver's fault. Dennis was riding a bike through a crosswalk that is poorly placed, that comes up quick at the bottom of a steep hill. Every week there was some accident or another. Plus, before speeding his bike into traffic, Dennis hadn't pushed the button to make the amber warning lights flash. Blame aside, the death of Dennis Miner, broken, limp and bloodied in the Geo's shattered windshield, touched a lot of people's lives.

The driver, who was never imprisoned and whose name isn't important, went stark raving mad after having stared into the dumb, broken eyes of that Miner, face all smashed and mottled with the crimson stuff of a pathetic life. This image had been forced on him. Shit sometimes happens. You don't get a say. Kids come flying through your windshield from all directions. You either deal with it well or you deal with it poorly.

The driver's name isn't important because it has been erased in the neighbourhood's history. He became "That Guy Who Killed That Kid." And I guess That Guy Who Killed That Kid couldn't handle it. In the end, he dealt with it poorly, weakly. I hear that his ten-year-old daughter found him in the basement, swaying from the support beams.

Way to be, Dennis. Beloved, foolish, fucking Dennis.

Beverly Miner, the mother, went nuts too. Mrs. Miner, unemployed and probably a little tipsy herself, was home to hear the clatter in the street outside: the thump, the screech, the shushing vacuum sound of a flame being extinguished. She pulled apart the curtain to see her son, curled up, so somnolent and sweet in the windshield of a Geo like it was a mother's lap. Dennis had been delivered right to her doorstep by the messenger of all that is unfair and fucked in the world.

Any mother would unravel, of course, except Bev Miner never

loomed herself back together. Cracked, she became convinced that Dennis's ghost was hunting their house, a shabby bungalow across the street from the Eddy Shack's Donuts where no one ever goes. I was never in the house, so I can only relate the build-up of detritus outside: a hodgepodge of car parts, baby strollers, a rusty gymboree and a college tuition's worth of empties, all denizens of their un-mowed brown swath of front lawn. To escape what she thought were the spectral whingings of her dear dead son, Mrs. Miner moved into the house next door, leaving their old house as it always had been, furniture and all, for Dennis to live in. The city footed the bill.

What a thing to do to your poor mother's nerves, Dennis.

And his death chapped my ass too. Pardon me for being selfish, but that happened to be my blue Raleigh he had been riding, stolen from the racks out front of Bogle Corbet K-8. I banged drums about the bike—I kicked up dust until you couldn't see your hand in front of your face, but to no effect. My loss was eclipsed by a so-called greater loss, which was eclipsed by an absurd campaign for canonization led by adults of Corbet who knew nothing about Dennis or the other Miner brothers.

The police impounded the bike as evidence. A kid was dead and no one wanted to talk about the fact that he had died drunk on stolen wheels and that he was an all around, irrefutable piece of shit. Living, Dennis was tolerated or ignored, but dead, he could get away with absolutely anything. His brothers enjoyed similar liberties.

If his mother was right and his ghost remains, as I suspect it does, not only in that dusty bungalow, but haunting everyone involved in the fiasco, it should know that I loved my beautiful bike. He owes me for the lock he smashed with a hammer, too. He owes us all so much.

I decided that Joshua was dead. There was no way that he wasn't. So I had a few selfish moments to commit our well-thumbed titty mags to the fire. Pornography was an element of the whole cruel show that I was in no mood to lie to adults about. Only after the porn was ditched did I pick up little Joshua in my arms, loving and tenderly as if he had nodded off in the backseat during a drive home from Toronto and I was his dad taking him up to bed.

Holding him out in front of me like an offering, I bawled and snivelled, dripping snot on him. Joshua was light, slow in growing. He had the sexlessness of a child who still smelt of his mother's milk. I walked through the mud puddles of the farmer's field, I didn't run. My carrying him had to be slow and dramatic and somehow triumphant. For the movie in my head, it had to beautiful.

In a half hour I got him to the dentist's house on the corner, a Greek man, Tsasis, who never tipped me when I collected every other week for the Corbet *Mercury*. Carrying Joshua for so long my arms had tired and I had no choice but to hold his slightness closer to my body, cradling him so my legs and torso could take the brunt of the weight. Joshua's head patted back and forth against my shoulder, muddying the sleeve of my shirt with a brown mess.

The dentist came to the door without a shirt on, only wearing his reading glasses and grey sweat pants with a hole in the knee. He had a fat gut and breasts that looked full and strong.

As the neighbourhood paper boy I was never allowed past the Welcome mat, but arriving with a dead friend in your arms is as good as an all access pass.

His house was the nicest I had been in. I stood among the sneakers and loafers in the foyer after the dentist had snatched Joshua from me, carrying him off to parts unknown, muttering *shit, shit, shit, oh, fuck, fuck, fuck.*

I walked through the house looking for the room where they had gone, gladly treading May mud on the carpet. Strolling, I took my time to inspect the artwork on the dentist's walls: bucolic renderings of boys resting with hounds by creeks and one glowing portrait of Jesus exiting his tomb. I leaned in to squint at the signature as if I might recognize the artist. The Greek's house was the sort where antique tables are there only to be discussed and where there is a room for entertaining that no one is allowed to enter.

Mrs. Tsasis had the car so we called an ambulance. Waiting for it to arrive, we washed the blood from my friend's blank face. Joshua was unconscious but still breathing calmly. The wound on his head, right beside his eye, was a gory patch of brown and purple with a small dollop of white bone in the centre. The gash aged him. He looked grown up now, mature. Sort of wise.

The dentist was livid, fuming, curling his bottom lip over his peppered moustache. "Who did this?" he demanded, suspecting, I'm sure, that it had been me. Wasting no time, I told him exactly who it was that had chucked the rock. I told him how they had laughed and what they had called us. How they ran and where they could be found—hiding out at 305, mind you, not 307. But when he heard their names the fury drained out of him and his tense face became doleful.

"Oh. Well," he said, sombrely and contemplatively petting the tangled, bloody hair from Joshua's forehead. Once fair blonde, his head was now swampy and dark, staining the dentist's lap. Looking from the living room, through the kitchen and out the back window, I saw the black plumes beyond the field.

I had failed to mention the fire and decided that I would not. If Mr. Cheapskate Fucking Tooth Yanker thought I had done this to my friend—because it sure wasn't the brothers of the martyr—then I would preclude any and all assumptions he might make about a flaming tree. I would not take any blame for those Miners and their cruel fucking grief violence.

"It's such a terrible shame," the dentist shook his head, his eyes getting glassy as if he was about to cry. "What happened to their poor brother. Only a child. It's just not fair."

No, dentist, no: it's *über* unfair.

When a child dies, his life is erased and becomes the property of the adults that survive him. All truth of character is obfuscated by the commiserative smog that a polluting community belches from their asses. No one is willing to celebrate the death of a cruel person so they excuse the shit and conjure a saint. Legerdemain.

Saintly Dennis Miner, who stole my bike, who stole all our bikes—who didn't even sell them or chop them for parts, but only rode them around for a day before ditching them in the Gimlet River—you will be sorely missed.

Saintly Dennis Miner, who knocked nests from trees and destroyed the hungry, cheeping skulls of baby birds with your saintly stone, just to see what their ruddy brains would look like smattered on the cement, we light candles for you and hold a vigil in the city square, singing hymns for the God that now holds you in his lovely, nesting arms.

Saintly Dennis Miner, who, in the hallway during a fire drill, anonymously punched me in the kidney and made blood dribble from the end of my penis like a weeping wound, you were too good for this world anyhow and we believe—we *need* to believe—that you are now in a better place.

Saintly Dennis Miner, who goaded Aaron, the autistic kid, into eating his own shit and to then hold the girls' heads between his fifteen-year-old vice grip, smooching them on their yowling mouths with his sloppy brown tongue, your spirit has diffused and now rests in all of our hearts.

Oh, you ubiquitous pig fucker so readily capable of such unmitigated violence, we gather in the gymnasium the day after your passing, all us kids who had been individually blessed by your grace. We stand with our false hands to our confused hearts and pray for you. We mutter along with our principal, Mr. Sharp, in a low, respectable babble. The division of church and state can go take a long walk off a short dock in these trying times.

During the service, your bereft brother Shane puts his palms to his lips, puffs his cheeks, and rips a big fake one that still echoes today. Cannon fire for a fallen hero.

Saintly Dennis Miner, the only miracle you ever performed was getting away with all of it and making it so that your wretched brothers could do no wrong, because you rode a stolen bike into the street and killed yourself, and no one with a dead brother could ever mean the nasty shit they do. The brothers of a saint seem divine by association.

Hallelujah and amen.

Joshua had ten stitches threaded through his bloody skin, spiralling like a hardball. He was severely concussed and had been only millimetres away from losing sight completely in his left eye. His parents, without accusing me directly, suggested that it might be best if I stopped stopping by. No one believed us. No one wanted to believe us when we said it had been Shane and Wayne. Cry, cry, cry. Fuck you all.

The next day Joshua wasn't at school to hang out with so I spent my recesses on the swings, lackadaisically drawing boobs in the damp sand with the tips of my sneakers. In class, I would look over my shoulder at Shane every now and again, and each time he was already bug-eyeing me, waiting patiently for me to turn, ready with a stuck out tongue or flipped bird.

I was willing to admit my position, stuck between a rock and a dead boy. I was ready to call it a day and get on with it when, in the last moments of afternoon recess, I heard a girl shrieking from over behind the baseball diamond. From where I was I couldn't see the girl. I could, however, make out the bleached mop of Shane's head bobbing up and down.

With a swoop of my foot I cleared my tits and crossed the playground. Reaching the gravel curve of second base I saw that Shane was on top of Julia McVey, a third grader girl, three years younger than him. His knees were dug into her shoulders. With one hand he had her nose plugged and with the other was holding her mouth open at the chin, spitting in her throat like it was a well. He wasn't laughing maniacally like a normal sort of mad person would but was filling her up with the atrocious concentration that some kids that age devote to long division.

When Julia cried and heaved I could hear, even from second base, the gurgle of Shane Miner's rheumy hork in her throat. Every time air passed through the skin of mucus there were sharp crackles, like wood burning.

I was not then, nor was I ever, a fighter. Physically I am awkward and not well suited for either combat or defence. I had, however, seen enough television brawls by then to know how the whole dance unfolds. Running like a shot, stealing home plate from second base, I ran up behind Shane, put the brakes on, and kicked him hard in the back, my foot flat against his spine, leaving a muddy footprint on his blue Budweiser sweatshirt. The force of my charge sent him over Julia, rolling his neck on the ground in a poorly executed somersault.

Julia wobbled to her feet and ran away sobbing, arms flailing. I jumped on Shane. Straddling him, I began to beat his purple face. A friend of mine who took karate had told me that to throw the perfect punch you must aim one foot behind the object you want to strike. In this way you punch clear through what you know to be your true target. So I concentrated on the earth beneath Shane Miner's skull and craved the treasure I might find there within.

The first punch I loosed foolishly from above with my right hand and hit Shane on the forehead. Immediately my hand curled into itself, feeling as if I had shattered every bone. Putting the pain aside, I simply switched—my clenched and manic left swung back and forth across his face, like a rowing pendulum. Blood from his nose and blood from his mouth, I broke skin above his eyebrow and let loose a further torrent. I burst his maroon pocket and it leaked over the rest of his dumb face. I cut my knuckles on his teeth. Bone against bone felt full and complete and just so fucking true. This violence was human and real. Tears of dreadful joy came. I was going for a complete fenestration of Shane's skull—if not to kill him, then at least to shed some light on his dark mind.

Let us be oh so fucking cruel, but never, never unnatural.

Julia returned, still blubbering and holding the hand of the recess monitor, Mr. Stephenson, who, arms underneath mine, pulled me from Shane. Interrupted, my fury detached from beatable flesh, I went limp and let Stephenson drag me back inside the school with his elephantine saunter.

He left Shane.

Stephenson turned his back and we walked away, leaving Shane Miner exactly where he lay, far out of sight from anyone else. Shane wouldn't return for last period, as he often didn't, and because his brother was dead and he was going through hard times, no one would search for him. He needed to take his time. Me, Stephenson, and Julia were the only ones who knew. It would be our secret.

I wanted Shane never to be found. I wanted him to be left there over summer vacation, unnoticed. In the fall he would be covered by the russet leaves, and eventually the cold ice and snow of winter. Come the spring, when baseball started back up, he would have disappeared entirely into the ground. The stink of thawed shit would be the only remnant of him.

I loved that porcine baldy for leaving Shane to choke in the mess of his own fluids. Though you could no longer see it, the blue ink splatter on Stephenson's belly was indelible. He didn't have it in him to forgive and forget like the rest had. Aching, stained paunches would not allow it.

At the very least I had broken the nose of a dead boy's brother. At the very worst I had broken his spine with my sneaker, or snapped his neck when I sent him overtop, killing him instantly. If so, all that time I had only been beating the life out of the already lifeless body of a Miner boy, stealing another one from his poor, haunted mother. He had gone limp and let it happen like the Miner's always did. Shane knew, in his stupid, self-serving way, that regardless of the outcome, dead or hardly alive, he would be the victor.

Nursing my right hand in a t-shirt filled with ice, I sat on the red plastic chairs in the main office waiting to be punished by the principal, Mr. Sharp. The head secretary, old Miss Morrow with the wispy moustache, kept looking up from her typewriter to shake her head at me, tsk-tsking my savagery. I couldn't help but smirk back at her. High on the wall behind her desk, enlarged and framed, was the grade seven class photo of dear and departed Dennis Miner, the patron saint of dead kids. This was the very same picture that had been printed in all the papers, which had been on the front cover of the Corbet *Mercury*, which I had delivered on time to the dentist's house only months before, and for which I had not received a gratuity.

Dennis' tussled brown hair was cut at the bangs, just above his eyes, and the long hair at the back flowed over his shoulders like overgrown weeds, snaking into the collar of his olive and salmon striped dress shirt. His mother cut his hair, no doubt. With one of his front teeth missing his smile was an unimpressed grimace, probably a response to a lame joke cracked by the Jostens photographer. The teeth that remained were yellow and had brown cookie between them. His nose and his cheeks were freckled like he had been sprayed with diarrhea from a distance.

The last part about this photo you had to be in the loop to notice. It wasn't so clear in the small pictures, but you could really notice it in the poster-sized version in the office. On picture day, Dennis had made a big to-do about writing *FUCK YOU* on his eye lids. Only that smartass had done it with pen in the bathroom mirror and it was backwards and smudged. That stupid look he has, the dim look of a weak flame, is Dennis trying to close his eyes in time with the flash of the camera. "Fuck you" was the message he sent out to all of us from beyond the grave.

Mr. Sharp's office door opened. He had loosened his tie and rolled up his sleeves past his massive forearms. He stood akimbo and cross in the doorway like he was ready to wrestle. Would there be mats, or would it be a street rumble? I was seasoned now.

Over the winter break, months ago, Sharp had had a stroke and now he drooped and wrinkled on the right side of his face. "You!" he shot his finger at me like it was a gun. "Ken! What you did. Makes. Me. Sick! It makes us all sick! Get … Get in here!" He scolded, shooing me towards him like I was a dog that had laid a coil on the front lawn, demanding that I scoot inside so he could beat me without the neighbours seeing.

A good boy, I stood up and walked into his room. There he was again: the hero, the victim, Dennis Miner, up there on the wall of Sharp's office. His half-closed eyes followed me on my way to an expulsion and a marred personal file, which, like a dirty conscience, was wiped clean a few years ago.

Fuck you backwards too, pal.

Beverly Miner eventually died as crazy old ladies tend to do, like a rumour going out of vogue. She was so far removed from the world that when the police went into her house to collect her body all they found in her cupboards, pantry and fridge was peanut butter. Supposedly she had been subsisting on the muck. After her death, Shane and Wayne Miner moved back in with their dead brother next door, living there for free, on Corbet's dime.

So. Shane is about twenty-two and Wayne is twenty-five. Last year they tried to rob the Eddie Shack's Donuts, the one where no one goes, with two kitchen knives. No masks, real casual, like they were running an errand. They absconded with what little money was in the register and crossed the street, back to their place to count it. There might have been enough for a bucket of chicken for dinner, maybe. They would lick their oily fingers and wipe them on their scrawny knees and thighs.

Crossing, I bet they were sure to press the button to make the amber warning lights flash, pointing their fingers to the other side of the road, right at their haunted house, like the sign says to. When the police knocked on their door to arrest them, the Miner brothers opened up willingly and politely. They shrugged their hunched shoulders and said that they weren't to blame.

Every year, on the anniversary of Dennis' death, March 21st, the city places a lovely wreath at the crosswalk in remembrance of the tragedy. Everyone knows, even the little kids that weren't alive when it happened, that that's the place where that guy got killed that one time by That Guy Who Killed That Kid.

Corbet has become a town of wreaths wilting in spring showers that turn the mud to shit, of adult women who refuse to go into basements, of broken locks rusting in the wet grass, of dried and crusting cum lines, of ink stains, of hearts clogged with peanut butter, and of burnt out fields where nothing more than suburbs will ever grow again.

That Ghost We Had

THE HOUSE WILL BE HAUNTED. There will be a ghost.

Anne had decided this their first July as husband and wife, soon after Eb began working the graveyard shift at the Wald plant. Coming out of the shower one morning, leaving dark and damp footprints on the bath mat, Anne stood naked and dripping before a cloudy reflection. With her finger she wrote *GET OUT* on the steamy mirror of the medicine cabinet. The fog would recede and the ethereal communiqué would disappear, leaving no trace. When her husband showered that afternoon before going to work—after she was long gone to the bakery—the warning would re-emerge. No mist would gather on the spectral demands and a queer message from an unknown place would appear to him, wanting to be acknowledged, wanting to be known.

Yes. They would be haunted.

There would be a third life in the house, creaking floor boards and doodling on mirrors. Anne and Eb would adopt their spirit as some newlyweds will a golden retriever puppy. If they worked hard at it, made a team effort, there would be this awesome ghost for them to call their own.

So then, the ghost would be a game. The only rule, Anne decided—while brushing her teeth and watching the letters disappear, bleeding into the mist, taking it over entirely until there was only her face in the mirror—was that neither of them would be allowed to talk about it. To speak of a ghost is to erase a ghost. It would not be permitted. If Eb ever asked Anne about the mirror dialogues she would become suggestively shruggy and aloof, rolling her eyes and biting her bottom lip, mumbling *Oh, you don't say*'s and *Hm, that's weird*'s. Eb would be confused at first, no doubt, as he was oft to be. But gradually, Anne was sure, he would glean the nature of the haunting and begin to play along.

Anne worked days, Eb nights. For that time, one was to the other only the shuffling sounds of leaving for work or coming home from work—soft music playing over breakfast at 6 a.m., or a muffled TV showing reruns of Leno at 4 a.m. The way Anne figured it, throughout the week they would communicate through their private phantom. It would be so cool. Every morning Anne would write something in the mirror, Eb would read it later and then write another spooky note for his wife to discover the following morning. The things they wrote would have to be eerie at first, of course, but over time, as the game began to make up its own rules, the ghost could write whatever it wanted to write. "Love yuh" or "Kiss Kiss" or "Out of milk, need eggs."

The ghost, the haunting, would be their *thing*. It would be their tacit, beautiful thing. It would take some getting used to, sure, but once they got into the swing of things the notes would become second nature. The gut of every couple, Anne figured, needed something coy and silly to define it. The ghost would be theirs to cherish like some couples cherish a song. Over time, it would become real—a spirit which existed in the lovely and unspoken nether-regional place between the two of them. This would be their charming, intimate haunting. It would be enough to get them over that first-year marriage hump.

Anne imagined that fifty years later, long after they would have forgotten about it, the no talking about it rule would become void. One day, eating breakfast together, their future children moved out and with families of their own, Eb or Anne would bring it up. Reaching far into the past, surprised by the memory, one of them would put down the paper and say, "Hey, do you remember when we were just starting out and doing that shift bullshit ... and there was that ghost. Do you remember that? Jesus. Wow. I'd totally forgotten about that. That ghost we had."

If plotted and executed properly, this ghost could be akin to finding a forgotten twenty dollar bill in your favourite jacket one spring when you could really use twenty extra bucks. The ghost would be so, so many things.

At first Anne loved this project. She was jazzed about it. For that whole first day, while kneading and baking dough, the ghost was all she could think of. The excitement she felt, the tingle, was a haunting inside of her—the ghost an Indian rubber ball thwacking and echoing against her sepulchral walls, waiting to get out, needing to be reciprocated. When she woke up the next morning she took a short shower, neglecting behind her ears and between her toes, so she could get to the ghost's new message quicker. She was sure it was there waiting. But, peeking out from behind the shower curtain, ready to be pretend terrified—a theatrical shriek or a dramatic, cinematic gasp and shudder—she saw only that same first message.

There, out of the steam, the curt demands of a ghost: *GET OUT.*

Anne tiptoed past Eb, zonked out on the pullout couch in the living room, and eased the door shut behind her.

So, he had not clued in. Anne left the initial words, there in the mirror, and waited. When, after a week, Eb's half of the ghost still hadn't shown up, Anne tried a new message. She wrote *LEAVE OR DIE*, doing the E's backwards the way she figured a for-real-ghost might.

But nothing.

Three days later, the next one said *THE HOUSE IS MINE.* The one after that, *I MOAN, MY BELLY SORE.* Still nothing.

In all this fake ghost stuff, Anne had managed to scare up a real ghost: a nothing that resisted wearing the suits she sewed for it, a nothing that would remain abstract and unresponsive. Just a horrible ghoul haunting the house.

The last message the ghost ever left was *MY SOUL REMAINS*

WEARY. That final warning, carved into the mirror's steam in daunting, uppercase phantom font, was never wiped off. The ghost's last words were there in the mirror every time Anne showered, staying with her as she dressed and left the house, always careful not to wake Eb, who slept on the couch so as not to wake her when he got home late.

MY SOUL REMAINS WEARY.

The house was haunted. There was a ghost. Anne understood well enough and it frightened her a little. But her rule was that she was not allowed to talk about it.

Flight School

I ONLY EVER SAW Tim's dad—Mr. Yendel—that one time when he came down to the basement where our detective agency was to get a tool to take back to his shed. Now, I'd say that he looks like that cartoonist, Crumb or whatever, but then … I don't know. Back then, I guess I'd say that he looked like Tim would probably look when he got to be as old as his dad. He was a stretched out version of his son. Tim was a lanky and sickly redhead with a hollow face who snuffled every time he pushed up his glasses, always with his ring finger, back to the brim of his big nose. He had those goofy kind of ears that were so thin and they stuck out so bad that they showed bloody tree branches every time the light was behind him.

Out there in the backyard under a big old poplar tree Mr. Yendel had this shed that he bought from some place out in Aberfoyle, just before the 401. He assembled it himself and then painted the shutters pink and the slatted body a dark brown, the kind of deep brown you'd never see anywhere in nature. The kind of brown that those plastic wiffel ball bats are coloured. When he came home at night from wherever he worked Mr. Yendel went straight to the shed where he was building his airplane. Not one of those big airbuses but the little kind with the propeller on the nose and only one seat. I never got a look inside the shed, no one did, but there was always hammering and the electric blue flicker of a welding torch in that tiny little window and then moments that were so quiet, when me and Tim would stop swinging and just be there on his rusty gymboree or whatever it's called and stare at the shed, waiting for some noise or other. But sometimes it would stay quiet until when the street lights would come on and I would have to go home.

Tim told me that his dad told him one time that when he finished the plane he was going to go to a school to learn how to fly it and then fly right out of there. But I don't know what happened with that because I stopped talking to Tim and stopped going over to his house when he stole my Ghostbusters car and then said that it had been his all along. The Ecto 1, and there was a guy inside. A Ninja Turtle, I think, but a guy's a guy. I tried to take it from him and he tried to strangle me, but then I kicked him in the stomach and took off without my car. I see him sometimes still, at ballgames or at the mall, and he sees me—he's getting taller and he's got glasses now exactly like his dad—but we don't say anything to each other or even look at each other because that's just the way it is sometimes.

Cocky Strides & Musky Odors

LINDSAY NGUYEN was swinging for the fences and clearing them—
scholastically. Linds works nights and weekends as a clerk at True
Value Hardware to help support her mother and older sister, a first-
generation immigrant and a paraplegic. She's not a vain smarty-
pants like some. She's just tooth-and-nail tough because—though
she can't control failure and success—laziness is not an option.
Weakness is not an option. And not only is she the smartest cookie
in Greenman's class, but Lindsay's also a decorated public speaker
with poise and elocution to beat them all. It was while she was
presenting her independent study report on *Notes from Underground* that something occurred to me about my own book.

I had read and was on deck to orally present my observations
on Chris Claremont's novelization of the *X-Men 2* screenplay by
Dan Harris and Mike Dougherty—which was based on a story by
Bryan Singer and David Hayter and Zak Penn. To distil the required
one thousand words of my written report, let's just say I argued
that the mutations which bring together the mutants are ultimately
what keep them forever at an arm's length from one another. The
X-Men are brought together by differences, for sure, but because
each of them is so defined by their own superheroic gene-distortion,
they will never be able to unite on the common ground of normalcy.
(It's a catch-22, which I've never read.) For instance, though Bobby
"Ice Man" Drake and Marie "Rogue" D'Ancanto have sloppy hearts
for each other they will never consummate their goo because Rogue
will drain the life force out of everyone she touches. Rogue's

mutation makes her a succubus and forces her to sit "a little apart from the others, as if she was wary of touching or being touched."

The essay I wrote was not bad, extrapolating the theme of loneliness and isolation as it pertains to the X-Men. I excel at this sort of work. That is, keeping my head down and farting along at my own gentle pace. When I have to be or care to be, I can be smart. Being smart is easy; you just have to prick up your ears every now and again and look up words that you don't know. But holing up in one's room and spouting this or that about this, that, and the other thing is vastly different than standing before a sea of bored peers with your dick waving in the wind, knowing that you're getting marked on poise and other hooey like that. So when Linds finished and my time came, I spat and I sputtered, using "um's" and "uh's" like commas. Nervous as shit, I recited directly from my essay and stepped in place like I was in an aerobics class that stressed the importance of subtlety.

I was so nervous that I completely forgot what it was that I wanted to say about *Notes from Underground* and *X2*.

"That will do, Mr. Blumenthal. Take your seat, will you?" Greenman was kind enough to stick his fork in me. Passing in the aisle of desks he grabbed my shoulder and said into my ear, "Hang back after class, okay. We need to talk."

So the mustard hadn't been cut. My presentation hadn't been up to snuff, as nobody says nowadays. "Nowadays," too, has fallen out of favour with the kids.

No one—except those drama club dinguses—likes presenting independent study projects and nobody even likes listening to them. Not even Greenman. For each presentation the student presenting swaps seats with the teacher. A big man, Greenman squeezes himself into our desk-chair combos while we go and stand in front of his oak desk at the front of the room. While Lindsay was presenting I snuck a peek over his shoulder at the evaluation sheet he was filling out. Doodling. That's all Greenman was doing. Inking little pictures of monsters like those gruesome rubber critters you used to put on the tips of your fingers.

So I flubbed the oral portion of the project and I assumed that Greenman wanted to hold me back to rap my knuckles and chew my ears about it. He would tell me that a book based on a movie was an inappropriate choice. To that I had planned to point out, as a joke or whatever, that Jer Wilkes had read *Clockwork Orange*, which was based on a movie too. But, no, Greenman wasn't so concerned about my academics. After everyone else had run out into the weekend he had me stand at his desk while he creaked back in his chair and put up his feet.

"You get high, don't you Joel? You're a waster, right? A pothead? A blazeoid? A... a *doob* smoker."

"I don't know what you're talking about, Mr. Greenman."

One of those "Mr. Greenman is my father's name" types who will cop out enough to wear a sharp teal dress shirt but will stick it to the man by wearing jeans and no tie and will roll their sleeves up past their elbows, he spent an entire class once explaining to us that hip-hop is the new poetry. And once everyone started shouting out names like *Snoop* and *50 Cent* and *Ludicrous,* he got red and livid and told us that we didn't know shit. "Shit" was exactly the word he used, trying to shock us. Didn't we know *Aesop Rock* or *Anti-pop Consortium*? What about *Fat Lip*?

Greenman likes to keep a trim black beard—with a dusting of white—to hide his double chin. "Fat" doesn't do such great justice to Greenman's proportions, but somehow gentle words like "chubby" or "husky" only ring true when you're talking about little kids. At Greenman's age what are you if you're not either fat or thin?

"Pot, Joel," he said. "Marijuana? Chronic? Don't treat me like a cherry, okay. I haven't always been your teacher, you know." And for a brief moment I took this literally and let my thoughts go. Because Greenman hadn't always been our teacher. He had arrived just two weeks before, when Miss Szabo took her maternity leave. Szabo was top shelf, a real sweetie.

Rail thin, pale and redheaded, she came to us fresh from teacher's college. Some redheads are messy with freckles but Szabo had a nice, sparse smattering. A hippie type, she wore flowery, flowing dresses and loose blouses with no bra. One afternoon, early in the semester, she took us out to the sports field to read *Sir Gawain and the Green Knight*. A downpour took us all by surprise and Szabo got soaked to the bone and continued the rest of the class inside. Her white blouse clung to her whiter skin like it was life.

At the time she must have been three or four months along. So her baby bump was slight but, with her doused shirt on her like Saran—wet wrinkles running all over it like veins—her belly was there to see in all its bounty. Her stomach was round, oval, almost like a third breast with her belly button sticking out like a nipple. Sitting there in my desk, it seemed soft and genuine to me: a place where you could curl up and lay your head. The sleep you'd sleep on that babyfull stomach would be long lasting and rejuvenating.

Szabo's breasts were like little chevrons, her nipples pink and unassuming. Greenman's breasts I've never gotten a good look at.

"Mr. Greenman ... I—"

"Joel, come on bud. *Jesus*: Kyle, would you? Okay? "

"Look, Kyle. I know what marijuana is, sure. But I don't do it." In truth, I was decently toasted right then. The period before English I had ditched art class to smoke away my pre-presentation jitters at my girlfriend Carol's. She's in university and has a basement apartment not too far from Wyndham High's downtown campus.

"Don't bullshit me, Joel. You think I can't smell the skunk on you? Look at those little pasties in the corner of your mouth. Don't bullshit me, okay?"

"So am I in trouble?" I asked.

"Well, that all depends."

"On what?"

"Thing is Joel, I'm new in town. I don't know anybody. You get it?"

"I don't think I do, *Kyle*. Get it."

"Okay," Greenman took his feet off his desk and leaned towards me. "Let me put it this way: If I were to do a random locker search— which I have the authority to do, by the way—and I just so happened to open up your locker, what would I find? Would I find enough weed to have you charged with possession? Or would there be enough in there to pin you with possession with intent?"

Finally I caught Greenman's drift: a plastic film canister about a quarter full was all I had in my coat.

"I don't deal, *Kyle*."

"That's a shame," Greenman sighed, leaning back again.

"I really don't have the time for it," I said.

"Sure. I understand. You kids have full, exciting lives. But can you score for me?"

"Ostensibly," I said.

"Jesus Tap Dancing Christ, Joel. Don't say ostensibly. Only dildos who want people to think they're smart ever say 'ostensibly'."

"Ostensibly's a perfectly cromulent word," I said. Greenman rolled his eyes like a drama queen. "Fine," I said. "How much do you want, *Kyle*?"

"An ounce should suit me for the time being. Just to see what your source is like. Then, if it's trustworthy, I'll probably get you to pick up more for me. Who's your guy?"

"Just this guy."

"Okay. I guess that's your business. So let's say you grab me an ounce and drop it by my place tonight. I'll pay you then. My address," Greenman wrote his digits down on a piece of paper and slid it across the table to me. His place wasn't too far from Carol's and it was an apartment.

"The thing is that I've got plans tonight."

Greenman got serious and started to finger his pout. "Joel?"

"Yes, *Kyle*?"

"*X-Men*?"

"Yes?"

"What the fuck were you thinking? Honestly."

"It's a good book."

"It's a movie, Joel. What happened to my copy of *Gravity's Rainbow*?"

"In my locker."

"Well I want that back. Pronto. Okay, chief?"

"*Clockwork Orange* is a movie," I said.

Szabo had approved my proposal to read *X2* before the winter break. She had encouraged us to choose books that were interesting to us and to use the oral portion of the assignment to communicate our own interests to each other.

"Joel, I don't want to be an asshole here—I don't want to harsh on you, okay—but I'm asking you to play ball. Really, I should flunk you where you stand for that sloppy stutter-fest you made us all suffer through today. And you're high. By not taking any action, I'm playing ball. Thing is I don't like playing alone. So how about you play some ball with me, huh?"

"I'll *play ball*? Okay."

"Cool beans, Joel. Cool beans." And Greenman held out his fist for me. Hesitantly, I bumped his knuckles and pissed off.

People rarely use "nowadays" and "hooey"—and ostensibly "ostensibly" is out of the question—but really, *cool beans*? Like the monkey that found a gun, Greenman must have picked it up some where and, not knowing what it was, started firing blindly.

My "source," as Greenman had insisted on calling him—like he was in a movie or something—was my pal Benny Nightingale. He scores for me from his older brother Karl. Sure, I could buy directly from Karl but the guy's a bit of a joke. When he was really young, specialists—doctor types and such—thought that he might have been retarded. Turned out that he was just a lazy flake from birth that eventually took to light narcotics like a hog to slop. If I can help it, I steer clear of the guy and stick with Benny. But Greenman had caught me on short notice and I couldn't tap him so late on a Friday night.

Karl lives with this junky girl in a two-floor deal downtown. The lore goes that the neighbourhood was built in the fifties to accommodate the mafia families that used to use Corbet as their base of operations outside of Toronto. Ostensibly, all the homes are connected by clandestine, underground tunnels where the Italian gangsters/family men would meet and plot their nefarious business deals and plan family barbeques. But now these dishevelled houses are mostly full of university students and fuck-ups like Karl.

"Well if it isn't William Wallace," he said, answering his door. Karl was buck naked and I had no idea what the hell he was talking about. William Wallace? His body is frail and flabby, a chubby sort of emaciation. His sculpted mess is the result of him being a guy that will lecture you on the benefits of a raw food diet while at the same time getting so blitzed that he will eat nothing but cookie dough for days and days and days. "Glad to see you, brother. Come on in. Take a load off. Make yourself at home."

His living room/"office"/studio is lit only by a few dim lamps, no overhead lights, and a gauze of pot smoke is always lingering like Scottish mist. A hodgepodge drum kit was set up in the corner with two microphones aimed at it and a few guitars were strewn over the floor with patch chords snaking out of them. Karl's a dealer but, like most dealers I know, he's also a musician. A musician with a big vision and a big plan.

His girlfriend was unconscious. She was naked too, splayed out on the couch with her arm up and hand covering her face. Her brown dreads were like furry clumps of stubby shit. She's some kind of artist. Her paintings are hung up all over the house. Mostly toothy vaginas and mopey self-portraits. Mostly crap. There is one that I do like, though. It's a picture of two clowns—Bozo and Cookie, if I'm not mistaken—in a boxing ring. The background is busy with celebrities like on the *Sgt. Pepper* album cover and flashbulbs are alive, lighting the clowns from all angles. Bozo's and Cookie's dukes are up, both of them have been knocked around and bruised already and both of them have raging erections.

An episode of the *Simpsons* was playing with the sound off on the big screen—the one where Homer steals sugar from a jackknifed sugar truck. Karl wrapped an earthy-toned silk sari around his waist and laid himself out on the opposite couch. The only place for me to sit was on the end of the futon where the girl was sleeping. I sat in the arch of her feet and shins. Her still toes and shins hugged around me. She stank of ripe B.O. and patchouli.

"Is she all right?" I asked, picking up her foot and letting the dead weight fall.

"Oh yeah. She's cool."

"Should we cover her up maybe?"

"Naw, man. Naw. It's cool. She's, like, a Mennonite. She doesn't believe in shame."

"A Mennonite?"

"Or a Buddhist or something. I don't know."

Karl picked up a pipe shaped like a penis—the shaft a shaft and the bowl the testicles—and started to cook it. The coffee table between us was littered with paraphernalia, mostly crunched up Evian bottles with fetid water at the bottom. There was a copy of the Upanishads with a cup ring on the cover. Karl took a long pull and then handed the pipe to me. "So, William Wallace, how've you been? Been a while, man. Been. A. Time."

"Sure has, *man*. But I'm good. Yeah. I'm good. You?" I sucked until it stung and the embers glowed a harsh red.

"I'm fan-fucking-tastic, man. Fan-fucking-tastic." I handed the pipe back to him.

Karl's not an especially good businessman. The only time I deign to buy straight from him is when I'm flat broke and desperate to smoke up. All I've got to do is say to him that I want to pick-up whatever amount and Karl will say "Cool, yeah. Take a seat. Let's chill out." And I can get rocked for free. When I get as far gone as I want to go I just say that I've got to hit the road. I leave as high as the noonday sun without having paid a dime. In a way, Karl's so lonely that he pays you to stay. But whether or not you give money to Karl, you always wind up paying in the end.

I couldn't stop staring at the clown hard-on girl like you can't help but staring at homeless people and deformed people in the streets. It's a sort of curious disgust. The more times the wang-pipe was passed to me, the more fixedly I ogled her.

"You like her?"

"What?" I said, startled, looking up.

"Kayla. You want me to wake her up? Maybe she'll want to have sex with you."

"No. I'm good thanks."

"Cool. Yeah. Just let me know if you do, though."

"Will do. But listen. I actually came over because I need to pick up."

"Cool. That's cool. What you need?"

"Like, an ounce I guess."

"That's cool."

Taking his creaky steps two at a time, Karl bombed upstairs. My eyes found their way back to Kayla and dallied there. I'd never seen a girl so blatantly naked. Carol always makes me turn out the lights and the girls in magazines like *Maxim* are professionally posed and airbrushed clean. When you grow up looking at magazine-perfect girls, the real thing can be kind of shocking. Kayla had yellow bruises on her shins and thighs and wore a curly black mess between her legs. Her stomach was bunched into rolls and there was the stippled shading of hair under her arm. Lying on her side, her one breast drooped over the other one like a lazy dog's ears.

Eyeing Kayla through the haze of Karl's dourly lit living room I started to think again about Miss Szabo and her wet blouse. Her nudity had been covered, but it was still there, right? Like looking at the sun through a shadow box. She had seemed then so clean. So perfect and fragile. Szabo wasn't ashamed of her body and she wasn't freewheeling with it either. Szabo was someone you could never touch for fear of breaking or bruising or tainting her somehow. Most other people I could knock down in the street and not think twice about. But Szabo was not most people.

With the stony fascination that once had me put my hand on an angry red stove element, I rested my open palm onto Kayla's bum cheek closest to me and pressed down hard, lifting myself off the couch and putting all my weight on to her. When I took it away I'd left a perfect maroon imprint of my hand on her sallow rump.

Karl came back down the stars slowly, folding up a paper bag.

"Hey William Wallace. Do you want to hear this new track I've been working on?"

"Actually, Karl, I've really got to be hitting the road."

"Oh, baw. Hang out for a bit and dig on this new shit I've been laying down. You kids are always in such a damn hurry. Don't realize how slow life actually is. Always rushing through it."

The real price you pay when you buy from Karl is that you have to listen to the album that he's been working on for the past five years. The title is *Dawn (With the Time's) Up*. It's a concept album, of course. He explained it to me the first time like this: "Well," he said, "the album's all about how, like, a beginning for one person is the end for someone else, you know? Like how when you're just starting someone else you've never met in your life is ending. Right? It's kind of like 'another man's trash is another man's treasure' except, um, you know." He's got a sketch book full of album art that's a hoot and a half. One cover is a bright blue sky over a cityscape at night. Another one is a skeleton cradling a baby. Yet another is a cowboy aiming a rifle at the sun. Karl did some and Kayla probably did a few too.

Karl crouched at the stereo to hook his four-track up to the speakers. "Have I played this new song for you yet? It's really new, so probably not. I recorded it the other night, like, in my backyard. I was on shrooms, right? And I just recorded this thing off the cuff you know, like all out of the blue and all, and shit, you know. When it's real it just happens, right? Like the really good shit you just can't force or process. Like raw food. So I did this and it blew everything wide open and now I've got this whole new angle and I've started looking at the album in a whole new way. Like a new vision, you know."

No. I didn't know.

He fast forwarded through a warble of other songs and as soon as he found what he was looking for, took a seat on the couch again. Karl lit a spliff, closed his eyes and settled in. After about a minute of tape hiss there was a loud clunk and muffle of a microphone being set up. Hiss remained, along with the thump of the spool turning, but now there was the nettling chirp of grasshoppers also. "Lo-fi ambiance" as my girlfriend, Carol, would call it. Another click came soon after, the sound of a second track being recorded. It was Karl breathing slowly and steadily through his mouth, sort of huffing, blowing into the microphone. A third track opened and as a guitar started to strum softly I figured out that the breathing was supposed to be some sort of a lethargic beat.

I'll admit it. I got lost in the track a little bit. But I was twisted by then. Blame that fascination on a ballsack stuffed with pot. It was still one of the stupidest, lamest things I'd ever heard in my life. Seems to me that you can do anything in a half-assed pretentious fashion—sober or looped—and get away with calling it art. Carol would disagree and I would disagree with Carol.

My eyes wandered to the TV. The sun was coming up over Homer's mountain of sugar. He had been guarding it all night with a baseball bat. Marge comes into the backyard and accuses him of being paranoid. He proves her wrong by reaching into his saccharine pile and yanking out some tea-sipping limey.

Unconsciously, but still aware of what I was doing, I began to whisper Homer's muted tangent: "Sure, I might offend some bluenoses with my cocky stride and musky odors. Oh, I'll never be the darling of the so-called city fathers who cluck their tongues, stroke their beards, and talk about what's to be done with this Homer Simpson."

The best lines from that show are the ones that have the least to do with the plot; the ones that make the least sense. The ones that have nothing to do with anything are the ones that have everything to do with everything.

In the song I caught onto another level of breathing. Then I realized that it was actually Karl in person, across the room from me. He had fallen asleep as soon as he shut his eyes. The smoke was pointed downwards and smouldering in his lips. Rising cautiously, I got up from the couch and took the joint from his mouth and pulled on it some before dashing it out on an upside-down CD on the coffee table. Body gone lax, his legs had parted and I glimpsed again, without meaning to, Karl's hairy confusion of genitals smooshed in between his thighs.

My hand print was starting to fade on Kayla's rump. Taking up Greenman's order, I closed the door quietly behind me as I left.

***

Greenman took his sweet time buzzing me up. A power trip, I'm sure. When he answered the door he was still wearing his teal dress shirt from earlier in the day except now the top three buttons were undone and it hung loose over a pair of grey sweatpants. His apartment smelt of sandalwood incense, bleach, and fresh paint. Like a teenager, Greenman had movie posters all over his walls. His were framed, though. A sign of maturity I guess. Ostensibly. There was *Rashomon, Down by Law, Jules et Jim* and *Reservoir Dogs*, all movies I knew because Carol had told me how important they were. And above his stereo system he had a long sword on display, sheathed in a faded blue case with golden swirls like an animated strong wind running along the length of it.

"Mr. Blumenthal, do come in."

"Here's your pot, Mr. Greenman," I offered from the foyer, not moving.

"Please, Joel. Please. Cut that crap." He already had a joint behind his ear like a tough.

"I got your pot for you, *Kyle*."

He snatched the paper bag from me and threw it on his coffee table. Like he had set them out to impress me there were copies of the *Paris Review, Harper's* and the *New Yorker* laid out. Theatrically exhausted, he fell into a lounge chair just beside the kitchen door and reclined, putting his feet up—warm in a pair of expensive looking moccasins—onto the foot rest. He blinked his eyes slowly, like they weighed a ton. From the glass of red wine on the table beside him, I guessed that Greenman had been getting sloshed alone, waiting for me.

"What do I owe you?" he asked. I made up a number that sounded high but not too outrageous and pocketed the bills. Getting an eyefull of Karl's schmuck, I had earned a little honest walking around doughsey-dough for myself. "Take a seat Joel. Hang out. Smoke this jay with me."

"If it's all the same to you I'd rather just split."

"What? You've got a date?"

"Actually I do."

"No you don't."

"No. I do."

"What are you Joel? Like fifteen?"

"Seventeen," I said. "Almost eighteen." It was nearly ten and Carol was waiting for me. She'd be pissed for sure and I'd catch it from her bad. I could have easily just turned heel and left except that I'd have to deal with Greenman on Monday and every other weekday until June.

"Whatever. You're young. Nothing you do right now'll count for a hill of beans in the long run. Cool your jets. Grab some couch, bud." Greenman pointed to the long, stark red leather couch with no arms that looked new like it had never been sat in.

Greenman warmed the length of the joint before lighting the tip. He sucked just past the paper twist and then held it out for me.

"No thanks," I passed, finally taking a seat. I didn't want him to think I planned on getting too comfortable. I was sure to leave my jacket and my shoes on.

"Joel, man. I'm cool, okay. This isn't a P.T.A. bust or anything."

"I know. I'm just good is all." Karl's wang-pipe still had me reeling and I couldn't stop thrumming my hands on my knees and walking my eyes around Greenman's. His colour scheme was warm, autumn colours: a lot of reds, oranges, yellows, and browns.

"Well chillaxe anyways. We'll shoot the shit. Do you want some wine?"

"Any beer?"

"Joel. What does this look like? A *kegger*?"

Greenman had a home entertainment centre that would make a techie cream his jeans. There was a big screen plasma flatscreen hung between posters, a DVD player, a VCR, multi-disc stereo, record player and different heights and widths of speakers smattered around the room like totem poles. His shelves dipped with the weight of too many CD's and DVD's. You can gauge a person's loneliness by how involved their electronics are.

"Do you like weapons, Joel?"

"Sure. I guess."

"Well. I'm against violence. I don't believe in it."

"You don't believe in it?"

"Yes. That's right."

Saying he didn't believe in violence was like saying he didn't believe in cars or smiles or oxygen. Stoned, I get finicky and literal. I was going to point out how stupid an opinion his was when he interrupted me.

"I don't believe in violence but I do find weapons very fascinating. I'm interested in how craftsmanship is used to obfuscate the actual design. The purpose. A piece of art that you can still run someone through with. That's a nice sword, isn't it? I saw you looking at it."

"Sure is. It's a beaut."

" 'A beaut?' What do you know?" With a few rocks for momentum, Greenman pushed himself out of his chair. Scratching his bum, he walked to the sword and took it down from the rack. He turned back to face me and slowly unsheathed it, kind of swaying his hips while he did. It occurred to me then, in my wild, skunky imagination, that Greenman might have brought me over to kill me or fuck me or something.

"This is a seventeenth-century Katana," he said. Greenman gripped the handle with both hands and held it stiffly out in front of him, angling the blade and squatting.

"That's Leonardo's sword," I said, saying it seemingly before I thought it.

"What?"

"In the *Ninja Turtles*," I said, catching onto my own point. "Leonardo's sword was a Katana."

"Fucking *Ninja Turtles*, Joel?" Greenman fell out of his samurai squat and let the sword go limp at his side. "This is an antique.

Okay? Expensive as hell. This sword was actually used by samurai in battle. People have died at the end of this blade, Joel. Can you even comprehend the gravity of that? The sheer force of life that's contained in this sword? Fucking *Ninja Turtles*? Jesus, Joel." Shaking his head he turned to his CD rack.

On the couch-side table was a framed photo of Greenman with his arm around some blonde. The two of them were looking coolly forward like they had better places to be. Both of them had cigarettes in the corners of their mouths and long-stemmed glasses in their hands. A wife? A girlfriend maybe? Judging from Greenman's apartment and track pants, whoever she was, she was an ex-something.

He put in a CD. It was stilted rock, something about viciousness, about being hourly hit by a flower. Gay parades. Except most parades are pretty gay, I think.

With the weight of the world on his round shoulders Greenman fell back into his chair. Staring at me through eyes that were becoming swollen and tight, Greenman took a few quick little tokes like the joint was burning hot and scorching his lips.

Greenman burned holes through me like it was my fault. Whatever it was. Everything was my fault.

"What kind of music do you like, Joel?" He said it like a challenge.

"I don't really like music."

"Loosen up, Joel. Jesus. I'm not grading you here. What do you like? Everyone likes music."

"Not me."

"Come on. Just name something."

"David Wilcox?"

"David Wilcox?"

"My dad listens to him. It's good I guess. I like that sometimes."

"No. Joel. David Wilcox is not good. He's pedestrian."

"Okay. Paul Simon, then."

"Fucking Paul Sim … What about this? Do you like this?"

"It's okay, I guess."

" 'Okay?' Joel? Do you know who this is?"

"Nope."

"Jesus. Don't you kids know anything?"

"I guess we don't, *Kyle*."

"This is Lou Reed."

"Never heard of him."

"What about The Velvets, huh? *The Velvet Underground*? You must have heard of them."

"Sorry."

Greenman was getting agitated, shifting in his chair. He started to clank the sharp tip of his blade on the glass coffee table. "Lou Reed, Mr. Blumenthal, practically invented rock music as we know it today. Punk music too. He lost it, I think, when he stopped using. *Blue Mask* was a piece of shit, really. But that doesn't matter. When he was at the top of his game he made an indelible mark on the history of music. He changed the world forever. You like *Green Day* probably. What? *Rancid*. I don't know. Fucking *Blink 182*, Joel? What exactly the fuck are you in to?"

"Those guys are okay I guess."

"Well those guys wouldn't even exist if it weren't for Lou Reed."

I turned away from the spleen in Greenman's dopey eyes and back to the picture. "No. They'd probably still exist," I stated distractedly. Both of them looked so excruciatingly awkward but they were still a match. They fit. In their pretentious, bitter way, they fit.

"What?"

"I'm sure that whether or not this guy ever made music has nothing to do with the fact that those people were born." The woman was pretty, her hair was shoulder length and swooped sharply down. Her bangs were hardly there. Inspecting closer, I'm pretty sure that her hair was dyed. She looked like she had gone to such extremes to appear sudden and incidental, whereas Szabo's flaming hair was always in step with how frazzled she was at that second. I would moon at her while she strove hard to explain an abstract concept to us, to put it plainly to us, her hand digging around her wild nest for a clear answer. Reading *Sir Gawain*, she had been so into it that she didn't even notice the rain at first.

Greenman clanked his sword harder on the glass, snatching my attention from the picture. "Fucking kids. You fucking kids think that everything was the way it is right now. That's a narrow, immature view, Joel. Do you understand that?"

"Okay, *Kyle*. Sure thing."

"You think you're pretty smart, don't you smart guy."

"I don't think that. No."

"Do you know what you are, Joel?"

"No, *Kyle*."

"You're a dirty nose picker," he said, pointing the tip of his sword at me. "Do you know how many kids pick their nose and eat their crusty, bloody, hairy snot? Everyday I stand in front of forty kids and this is all I see. The only thing I've learned in all my years of teaching is that everyone is a dirty nose picker when they think no one is watching. Joel, that's a terrible truth. And I've seen you do it to, smart guy. I've seen you finger it out and then stick it right in your mouth."

"I know that I pick my nose, Mr. Greenman. I do it when I'm thinking."

"Take off, Joel." He closed one eye and held his katana straight at me, angling me right in the movie he was making. "You're dismissed."

I split like pants.

In the ten hours since I had last seen her, Carol had shaved her head and adopted horn rimmed glasses like Buddy Holly. Sometimes she goes on about being bi like she'll rattle on about important bands and books. Carol doesn't shave her legs because she's a feminist—her word—but she gets electrolysis done every few months to keep her eyebrows sleek. And even though she's *totally* against materialism, Carol owns two dozen pairs of shoes, a baker's dozen of which are Chuck's. All the colours of the rainbow. A Con for every occasion.

Believe me, if bashing out all of your teeth with a rock was "in" then Carol would no doubt be as gummy as my grandmother.

I let myself in without knocking and threw my coat on her desk chair. Playing on her laptop was some racket of sloppy drums and searching, worse-than-beginner electric guitar. The singer, his voice wobbly and tortured, was talk-singing some bullshit nonsense. And of course an ambient lo-fi tape hiss drenched it all like rain. Cacophony is the appropriate word, I think. And Carol was lying on her side reading a book under her sole lamp. Her brown cords were second-hand faded and her *Jurassic Park* tee had probably belonged to me when I was seven years old.

With my back to her I sat down on the edge of the bed and toed my off sneakers. "What *are* you listening to?" I asked.

Her apartment is one cold, long space beneath an old Italian couple who fuck like squirrels. Downstairs always smells of the thick aroma of sauces that the Italians above are always making when they're not making love. Carol's accoutrements are sparse: just a desk beneath the one window in the corner with her computer on it and her bed against the back wall. No shelves. Instead, Carol likes to stack all her books along the wall like she's in some Russian hoosegow. Goulash, they're called. Make no mistake about it, her parents keep her pockets full of dough. Squalor is the lifestyle she chose. She keeps her walls bare except for a few pinned-up art-print postcards: some Modigliani nudes and one Magritte of a woman's face as her torso—that is, boobs, belly button, and crotch where eyes, nose, and mouth would be.

Carol doesn't have a TV because she doesn't believe in it. TV is the new opiate of the people, she says. She doesn't have a proper set, no, but Carol downloads shows and movies on her computer like crazy.

"About time," she said, chewing a pen and not looking up.

"What is this?" I asked again. The music was getting worse, sounding like drunk children let loose with their parents' tape-recorder.

"This is *Jandek*," Carol said like I should have known to hear it.

"What-deck?" I asked.

"*Jandek*," she said again, huffing then tsking. She put down her book and sat up. "He's this guy from Houston, right? Total recluse. Completely underground. He's never played a show and he's never even been seen. His albums just appear out of nowhere. Total mystery."

"He's retarded, right?"

"You're retarded, Joel. It's art, okay."

"Sound's like shit to me," I muttered under my breath.

Carol crawled to me like a cat across the bed. She's the same size, ostensibly, as she was at twelve, only just above five feet. She pecked me on one cheek and smacked me on the other. "That's because you're a philistine."

"I'm more of a filibuster, really," I said

"Don't be a fuck," she cuffed my head hard and threw herself back onto the bed. "So what was the hold-up? There was other shit I could have done tonight."

"School stuff," I said, lying down, my head at her waist, looking at her upside down. Karl's smoke was spiralling out of me like water down a drain and was taking my energy, like soapsuds, along with it. I closed my eyes and felt swaddled.

We work together at Winners, Carol and I—cashier and stock boy—and make mocking, goofy eyes behind the backs of the lame-wads that buy granny panties and lingerie. Like we're better than them. On good days, according to Carol, I'm mature for my age. But when I disagree with her or roll my eyes at some of the highfalutin' opinions she can rattle out I'm *im*mature and will only get "it" when I'm older. Books, for instance. Carol's into books about nothing that go nowhere. Over and over again she explains to me that books with plot—that is, books with anything at all interesting happening in them—are not in touch with the way the world really is. Art, according to Carol—which means according to one of her professors—is a mirror meant to reflect the true nature of nature and our place in nature. Or some such baloney.

At twenty-four, admittedly, she's robbing the cradle and at seventeen I'm robbing the grave. Like I said, I'm smart. I know exactly why Carol wastes her time with a wet-nosed pup like me. We don't date, like dinners and movies or walks by the river in autumn. We're casual—or "cag'" as Carol got to saying for about a week, the "g" soft. Sometimes I go over to her place and swallow the dirt from the cultural holes she's been digging until I've paid dues enough to move on her. And after that it's between us and the sheets.

And look: I've got no bones about any of it. That it's better to give than to receive is a keen enough idea, good to sell holidays, but that's not how human transactions go down. It's taking. It's all taking. Everyone's a user. The lion's share of folks, at least. I'm not talking savage thieving, but a laidback allowance of back and forth B & E.

Carol uses me to be everything that she wants so badly to be. She wants to be smart and sexy and worldly with her finger on the pulse of the underground. She can't sell that with her friends—Carol has none—so puts on the show for me, a young boy who knows no better. And I five-finger her right back.

"Are you sleeping?" she scolded. I had dozed off.

"No," I said, opening my eyes and propping myself up on my elbow. "I'm here."

"How did your presentation or whatever go today?"

"It went okay," I said, lifting her shirt to sneak a peek of her navel. A little trail of dark down criss-crosses like baseball stitching and disappears under her belt.

"Lay off, buddy," Carol said, both serious and joking, taking my hand away. "So I was reading Barthes' *La Plaisir du texte* today."

"What?"

"The *Pleasure of the Text*."

"Oh, of course."

"You probably don't know it."

"Sure I do," I said. "I read it all the time. I read it on the can, like, all the time."

"Shut up, Joel. It's so way, way over your head."

"I'm sure it is."

"Barthes says, right?, that the *Pleasure of the Text* isn't like a striptease. Right? The pleasure of reading's not about narrative suspense, okay. He says that it's not about waiting to see the tits or waiting to see who the murderer is."

"Then what's it about?"

Carol's stopping to think gave me enough leeway to pull her shirt up high enough to spy one milky slope of breast. "Fuck off, Joel," she smacked my paw and covered herself. "There's no point in trying to explain anything to you. You're so closed-minded. Like, you think that you understand everything, so anything you *don't* understand must be stupid. And that's *so* stupid."

"No. No, tell me," I pressed. I crawled up to Carol and hovered over her. "I want to know what reading is *all* about. Enlighten me."

"Piss up a rope, Joel." Carol was sulking.

"I will. But after you tell me all about why Bart thinks I don't read right."

Moving on her served my wants but it also rescued Carol from the hole she had dug for herself. I'm a nice guy like that. Never a fan of having me in a superior position to her, Carol rolled me over. Something jabbed into my back and, reaching beneath me, I pulled out—wouldn't you know it—*Notes from Underground*. No fooling. Carol tossed the book aside and put my hand on the small of her back. But seeing it was enough to jog my memory.

I tried to hurry her shirt off, but she rolled away from me and turned out the light, exposing herself without letting me see.

"Males are visual," Carol always assures me and goes on to insist that she understands my want to keep everything bright. "But tough tits," she says, "the lights stay off." Some people never grow out of childhood mentalities, like when your friend will always insist on playing only at his house. It's so he can make up the rules. His house means his rules.

So I have no choice but to imagine for myself, giving Carol the body of any number of Maxim girls. Which is fine, except that now and again, soaked Szabo will be there in my imagination. When she comes along I freeze up and go slack.

"What's wrong?" Carol breathed, with a rare glitch of worry in her tone.

"Nothing," I said. "It's nothing."

Carol's as cold as I am. We bandy sarcasms back and forth and shirk seriousness at all turns. We two have tough skins and can brow beat each other black and blue. But when it gets late, when clothes have come off and we've taken all we care to take, Carol's ice melts and she becomes so soft and scared. She shrinks almost. I don't know how to say it better. She shuts up and she hugs into me. And if I roll over she won't let me go, like an attention-hungry dog that will force its head under your hand when you stop petting it.

Some people clothe themselves in so many layers, like they're always dressing for a day of uncertain weather. Carol wears her glasses, her cardigans, her little-boy shirts, her striped leggings, her jeans, her Cons, her books, her movies, her music and her theories. I think her worry—not to get too far out there or anything—is that when she removes all those layers there will be nothing left underneath. Just one big empty. And when she holds me I can't help but feel like she's only trying to put me on like all those other things.

And it's then, only then, when Carol gets loose with her loneliness and fear—when she turns into me, needing me—that I ever get afraid. With anything else, I can mock it until it means nothing and I feel like I've got the world wrapped-up.

When Carol spoons me she puts her lips on the nape of my neck, resting there and breathing there. The smell between us is salty and musky. She presses hard into me, her breasts smooshing between my shoulder blades, making little warm spots of sweat, and she winds into me like ivy up a trellis, her legs hooking into mine and her arm snaking under my armpit and over my chest while she strokes my cheek. Her breath smells like stale cigarettes and plaque. And I can't make a snide comment about it. She's dressed down so completely that I can't possibly dress her down any more. Now the panic sets in like a grass stain.

And while she turns to me, maybe, for safety, Carol's not someone I could ever drape over me to keep off the storm and cry like a stupid baby with until the weather lets up. It's ugly, but there it is. It's in these moments of panic and vertigo that I let Szabo come freely into to my frantic thoughts. Along she comes to me and I rest my head on her soft, pregnant belly where I fall asleep so easily while she pats my head, telling me over and over, whispering, that it will be okay, that it will be okay, that it will all work out hunky-dory in the end.

But the bridge. Let's not forget just because I had forgotten before. I'll be brief.

Now, I've never read *Notes from Underground*, but I feel that I can speak freely and knowingly about it. Carol does it all the time, passing judgments on books she's never read. Linds Nguyen I trust. I trust that with her straight teeth and sharp nails she chewed and scratched to the core.

Eric Lehnsherr, a.k.a. Magneto, is the primary villain in the *X-Men* movies. The novelizations, too. The germ of his beef with humanity goes back to his time spent in a WWII concentration camp. From there, as he grows and discovers the power that is his mutation—an ability to control everything magnetic—his rancour escalates thanks to humanity's coldness towards mutants. Where Professor Xavier and his X-Men grow compassion in the face of this coldness, Lehnsherr grows only greater hatred and hubris. This rage climaxes, in the first movie, with Lehnsherr building a contraption that would, ostensibly, turn all people in the vicinity of Liberty Island into mutants. The X-Men, thankfully, put a stop to that bad business. As a punishment, Lehnsherr is imprisoned and rendered powerless in a plastic cell in the centre of Mount Haven, which is where the second movie/novelization picks up.

And it was this that I thought of while Linds was eloquently going on about her *Notes from Underground*.

Similarly, the speaker of *Notes* is imprisoned underground—self-imprisoned, I gather—because of his spite towards his fellow man. Both these old bitchers are trapped, powerless in their solitude, harping on the ways of humanity, reducing everything to over simplified categories. What Magneto fails to realize, though, is that if he had succeeded in mutating everyone, he would have gotten nowhere. Because, as I argued in my essay, the mutants themselves—though ideologically tight—are physically and genetically separated by this rift.

It's only our differences that make us lonely—shut away in our respective mountains or mouldy corners. Magneto and Mr. Notes refuse to put up with other people's bullshit and take their own bullshit to be right and true. They expect everyone to meet them on their level, to come into their solitary confinement where they can turn these guests into bastards as sad as these sad old bastards are.

The only difference, really, between the speaker in Notes and Magneto is that Magneto is powerful enough to manipulate the magnetic field of the earth itself. Ostensibly.

Now Watch This

THIS SUNDAY AFTERNOON Ev took me fishing. We went to a pond he knows about, on the outskirts of town, just down the hill from the county's correctional facility. We rolled up our jeans and sunk our feet in the water, shading ourselves from the high sun under drooping willows—drooling willows almost—that leaned so far over the bank like they were thirsty. We balled up our socks and stuffed our shoes. All weekend he's been wearing his new soccer cleats to break them in. Seeing his small cleats beside my big Vans reminded me of the time, in the delivery room, when I first fit my thumb into his tiny palm. My first thought was not how small he was, but how big I actually was.

Across the pond, past the gravelly, unkempt ball diamond, the correctional facility loomed like an old world castle. Ev said that he could hear inmates shouting. I told him that he was imagining things.

"Did you hear it that time? Some guy just shouted 'You're all gonna pay.'"

The only catch in that roily brown water were catfish and what Ev calls rainbowfish. These are two of the ugliest fish I've ever seen up close, held in my hand, eye to eye. They must be dim to boot, because they're a cinch to catch. You simply have to jerk your line and they hop right onto your hook like submerged divers, looking for treasure. You tug again and the dim fish tug back, giving the signal that they're ready to come back up, booty in tow.

Landing a catch in that pond was simple as shooting fish in a barrel.

I could have caught a truckload of these dumb, ugly fish and still I don't think Evan would have been honestly impressed—though he played the part—because he knows how easy it is. That's exactly the reason he brought me to that pond and not somewhere else.

We threw most of the catches back because it's not like we're going to eat them. The only fish we kept was the first one I caught, the cat that I hooked right through the watery, emotionless eye, killing the brain. This is the one that we will dissect with a steak knife on our back deck.

Afternoons like this one are great. We are father and son in the most soft and blatant Andy of Mayberry sort of way. That I think fishing is slightly lame doesn't matter, because it's for him. We made sandwiches and we tried to explain the music we like to one another, there under thirsty willows with the correctional facility rioting in my son's imagination. Somehow Ev's gotten into the Talking Heads and he's affable enough to listen and nod when I try to extrapolate hints of Clash influences in his Green Day tapes.

It's not that I don't enjoy the challenge and effort of meeting him halfway, but by far Ev's Wednesday night soccer games are tops, a breeze. My only responsibility is to make sure I get him to the field on time and remember to bring the orange slices that Wendy cuts up when it's our week. Wednesday night asks nothing of me. The game starts, I slip into automatic father mode, and I raise my voice and lose my head.

"Go Domino's Pizza!" I scream, like an inmate.

Wednesday night soccer games are a scene of endless pride and quiet disappointment. On the sidelines—they sunken into their plastic lawn chairs and me who is fine standing with my hands in my pockets and my nose in a book—I smile at the other fathers. Every week I see these men, nod to them, but don't know any of them from Adam. And, really, I don't care to know squat about them. To each other, we're nothing more than men with boys.

The first few games I hung back and watched, probably seeming like Ev's indifferent stepfather or his mother's new beau, maybe. I held my tongue until I gleaned the script well enough to submit my own *Atta boy's!* into the cacophony of the game. I wanted to be sure that the other players wouldn't make fun of Ev because of me. Now, when I get into game, I feel brave and anonymous, laying low in the bedlam. The parents yell, the kids yell. Everyone yells.

Last week, one of the fathers—Ted, maybe—came up to me after the game. Out on the field, the two teams filed by one another, shaking hands, muttering *good game, good game, yeah, yeah, good game*, to each other. Ted snuck up while I had my nose in Blake and he frightened me. I'd done nothing to deserve a conversation. I was at the point in *The Marriage of Heaven and Hell* where, after having visited an infernal print shop in hell, he picks up with an angel and regards the abyss. Suddenly, Blake finds himself on a moonlit river bank, listening to a harp. The harpist sings, "The man who never alters his opinion is like standing water, and breeds reptiles of the mind."

"You're Evan's dad, huh?" Ted said outright, scratching his temple sheepishly. "Yeah, sure. Good kid. Helluva a player, huh? Yeah. Probably the, uh, best player on the team, eh? You must be really proud."

"Oh yeah. Holy shit, yeah." I rolled the book and put it into the back pocket of my jeans and lit a cigarette. "Your kid's really great too, man. Gotta whole lotta hustle. That's what really matters." Except, Ted's son, I'm now pretty sure, is the one fat kid on the Domino's Pizza's who, when he runs, wheezes, hiccups and let's his wrists flop.

This week Ted didn't even look at me. Of course he knew I was bullshitting him when I muttered that bunkum about the hustle and this week he ignored me completely. I should have said something more like, "Your kid's really smart. He knows his own body well enough to know he'll drop dead if he runs too much, so he always dallies around in front of the other team's' net. The other dads, between you and me Ted, call your kid a cherry-picker behind your back, but I think that's really keen of him. That's what I'd do:

stand and wait in front of the net until the ball comes to me."

Individually, on the sly, they confide in me that Evan is the best player on the team. And that I should be so proud. And I am proud. Holy shit, am I ever. I glow like any good pop would, but at the same time I'm scratching my chin over how the hell this happened. Ev sure doesn't get this stuff from me. In his navy blue shirt with red trim and a stiff, plastic number 8 on the back, he charges around that field, knowing the lithe dance moves that boys his age are allowed to know. Ev's got steps of stealth and he kicks the ball between his feet and then through the legs of the other kids who he darts in front of to get back the ball—*deek, deek, twirl, deek*—and then he hoofs that checkered world so far, using the inside of his foot, and it goes flying with this precise arc. The trajectory is beautiful. It's one of those perfect things that occur in nature sometimes.

Had I taught him soccer, I would have told him to use his toe because it just makes sense. To me at least. But Ev knows better. Somehow he knew to know better.

And man, that kid can tear back and forth across that field, chugging his legs and pumping his arms. His cheeks flush like mine do when I climb a flight of stairs. Always he has this serious and almost pious look of concentration. Dancing and hopping, he jerks his neck, flicking his long, jock-star blonde hair out of his eyes without missing a beat. I've never known a kid to love running so much, to love being swept away into the fast current of the game. On the sidelines, on the bank of that crazy river, my only obligations are to hoot and hoot and hoot, to give in to the communal insanity, forgetting myself in him and letting Ev know that I'm there and that I love that he loves it so much.

Ev might be the best, like the other dads say. I don't know. I have no idea what goes on at these soccer games, with all the whistles and flags and other fathers groaning about something, secretly disappointed by a bad play their kid made. And I don't care what happens in the game, really, just so long as no one messes with Ev.

Once, another kid, the best player on the team with the red jerseys, the Tim Horton's—the ones who were losing—kicked Ev in the shin on purpose. Everyone on both sides saw how heinous and wrong that was. Those sitting rose from their lawn chairs to get a better view of the foul. A few parents hissed at the aggressor. The ref had to stop me from charging the field.

While Ev calmed himself and took his penalty shot, I was stewing under my shady maple tree, by the trash can orbited by bees. Put off to the sidelines, I could see that little bastard snickering around with his team mates. Laughing it up, I'm sure. Not paying attention to Ev's penalty kick, I was imagining all the intricate ways I could kill that twelve-year-old showboat. It wasn't movie violence I dreamt, but limbic, ancestral savagery. These were fantasies I didn't know I had inside me.

I would wait for that gloating fucker in the parking lot, pretending to be a scout maybe. Leading him away to discuss contracts, I would kick him in the back of the legs, dropping him. Then I would stomp his face into miscellany with my clunky Vans. And then while he was down but still breathing, I'd take the car over him and break him in half. Or I'd do it quick with a stone to the side of his skull. Or, with my hands around his twig neck, I would know precisely which tube to place my thumbs over in order to finish the job. I would know how to hug around his head and snap him. And I wouldn't be sneaky about it. I'd showboat the murder and do all the time in the world for Ev.

Without ever having hit anyone in my life, or having seen deep, black blood up close, I knew exactly what it would be like to murder that boy. And never had I felt so much like Ev's actual father. I could handle everything because I knew, then, that there was this secret man born inside me on the same day as my son was born.

When he was a baby, Wendy and I read Blake's *Songs of Innocence and Experience* to him every night, holding up the engravings for him to see, hoping to inspire in him an early brilliance from the get-go. I was still playing in The Gallimaufry when he was small, and I would bring him to shows. And though I don't play much these days, he still loves tagging along.

But Ev didn't want to do guitar or piano and it's a battle to get him to read a book. For the longest time, sure I was a little disappointed that he didn't come out quite as I'd hoped. I felt the way the other dads would probably have felt if their boys wanted to study the cello. But now, every time he gets that ball I go so fucking nuts. I'm sure Ev knows that I'm amazed and I'm sure that he knows I don't understand. But now and again, when he's on a breakaway for the net, he'll look up at me, and he'll give me this vexed smile that says, *Holy shit, Dad, can you believe that I can do this? This is so crazy. Now watch this.*

We spread out the Saturday funnies and splay the brain-dead catfish on the patio table. The only surgical tool that Wendy will let us use is an old steak knife. Carefully, wearing a pink gardener's glove, I carve the ugly fish under the chin with the serrated edge, if fish have chins, and all the way down the amber, scaly belly stopping at what could be either the hole where it shits or pisses. The guts, muddy and dull lavender, ooze out onto Calvin and Hobbes and Far Side. The innards seem so unspecific, crammed in all willy-nilly. Ev lights up and whispers *wow*.

"I think the big sack, the blue-ish one, is the stomach," Evan says, tracing a few inches above the gore. "Can I cut it open and see what's inside?"

"Which one?"

"That one there I think." Ev points to a soft, oval organ and I hand him the gardening glove and then the steak knife. With his soccer player's concentration he makes a parabolic incision. At first, when it's punctured, water weeps out of the sack and dribbles onto his emerald Umbro shorts, but he doesn't flinch. Evan waits patiently until the flow stops and then he continues, breathing slowly and seriously from his mouth like he does when he sleeps.

Ev is right, this is the stomach. He opens it up completely and shows me the contents, the last things the catfish ate. These are the four things we find inside: three stubs of primary colour Crayola crayons, and a pristine dime from 1982, the year Ev was born.

"That's so messed up," Ev gawks. "How do you think all that crazy crap got in there?"

"I don't know," I hum. I think about it for a second, and then a second more. Coming back from the pond, we had passed the correction facility again, and Ev asked me what the difference was between a prison and correctional facility. I could only admit then, like now, that I didn't know.

"Really," I say now, "there's no reason at all that money and crayons should be in a fish's belly. It's impossible. Sometimes there're just these impossible, really specific things that happen that, even when you try hard, you'll never be able to explain. Impossible, but look: there it is anyway."

Ev rolls the dime between his thumb and index finger, still wearing his surgical glove, and holds it up to the afternoon sun. The stomach acid has to be what makes it look so shiny and new.

Jellyfish Bites

ON THE BEACH, Eric and Erica—the neighbours, Ted and Nina's twins—were twirling sparklers, spelling out their names. A chamber piece before the orchestra, the big cottage country fireworks show.

In glowing, red cursive Eric managed to sustain his in the black-eye blue dusk. Erica could only spell her brother's name before the E faded, just as she finished her a.

I took a picture of their sky graffiti, letting the shutter linger open, capturing their trails and blurring their arms.

The screen door clapped shut. With a sippy-cup of whiskey old Tom Jod' lumbered out. Heel to toe, she walked to me as if on a tightrope, gracelessly. My family's cottage has a grassy backyard that bleeds into a pebbled beach on Lake Nipissing. Built by hand at the turn of the century, the cottage smells always of thunderstorms. Before Jod' it was my daughter Beth that I would spend the summers here with. But those two never got along—it's impossible to get Beth in the same room as Jod', such strong personalities the both of them.

She straddled the picnic table bench beside me. Jod' had put on a black sweatshirt over her one-piece bathing suit—a ratty old souvenir from Alberta with silver wolves howling under a silver moon on it.

"You know," she said, settling her feet into my lap, "there's this baby in my stomach."

Jod's eyes were on the twins, her stare droopy, her breathing stertorous. At first, getting Jod' to come along was to move heaven and earth. She complained about the heat, about the coppery water. But when the twins were born, she made less of a stink.

I pulled my sweater over her feet. They were cold and callused pressed flat against my stomach.

"I've always felt full. And that's not a fat joke. It's always been in there. In here. This loaf. It has no form or anything. Just a lifeless blob of potential." She curled her toes into my belly fold, gripping. When she flexed them straight again her big toe scratched the underside of my breast.

"And I've decided to name that lifeless blob after you, Barb."

I aimed the Minolta at her, but Jod' put the sippy-cup out to block.

"You could have had kids," I said, putting down the camera.

"Me having kids would be child abuse." She took a noisy slurp.

No child should have to grow up with a fat and ugly mother, according to old Tom Jod'. That's what she calls child abuse. It didn't take me long to realize that on this point she was unmovable.

"You know I hate it when you say that," I said, not needing to add that Jod' didn't know shit from Shinola when it came to child abuse.

To assure her that she's not fat and ugly is pointless. Jod' the Toad was her nickname as a child. Sure enough, Jod' is squat and wide, though more akin to a bullfrog, really, what with her prodigious double chin. Her eyes are long and squinted so that everything seems far away and impossible for her to see. Behind her thick lenses her eyes are magnified into what Jod' calls her "two blind cunts."

Worst of all, at fifty-seven, Jod's russet, frizzy hair is thinning and already she has a noticeable bald spot. As balding men will, Jod' resolved to shave her head this summer.

"Nope," she said, not looking at me, but past me, "everything was denied me from the word go. Too much of a hag for kids, too much of an ugmo to land a man, even."

"Shut-up," I said, a little quiver coming into my voice.

121

"No. You shut-up your pretty mouth, Barb."

Screams from the beach. High-pitched squeals of frightened excitement. One was chasing the other. At ten, Eric and Erica are still mostly indiscernible. The two of them shriek equally like girls and rumble equally like boys.

"Women like you float effortlessly through life like a ghost goes through walls." Jod' sucked at the tip of her cup. "You floated through a husband, you floated through motherhood. You fouled those up and now here you are, unscathed, going easy through me. All because you're easy on the eyes, Barb. Lookers, they can do anything because they're... Inoffensive.

"But me, darling, I'm an abomination."

When I met her in the late '70's she was making her living as a portraitist—Jod carved busts into tree trunks. She was a known character in Toronto art circles, famous for being an acerbic snob about who she would render. She would only have especially beautiful women sit for her. After all our years together, she finally did me a few summers ago in the cottage's backyard, on the old oak stump that has always been used as a chopping block.

Though the portrait was hardly flattering, more a condemnation—with such ire and envy did Jod' affix my face to that chopping block.

Today Jod' will raise the axe high above her as she separates the logs for our fires. When she's done, with a final burst of strength, she plunges the axe down so deep into the oak that only she's strong enough to wiggle it free again.

Now the twins were roaring and snarling monsters. With arms raised high and with claws out, they stomped with plodding Frankenstein feet towards each other. When they tangled they slowed their motion for a cinematic row, thrashing and clashing, drawing out their howls. I can remember sitting at this same picnic table, ages ago, watching their mother Nina and my Beth, darting and leaping, into and out of the water. Sometimes Nipissing would be a lava flow. Sometimes they would save each other and sometimes both would perish, sadly, together.

Old Tom Jod' sparked a stogie. Her face lit up in the sulphur flare. A coca-smelling plume floated out of her mouth.

Since our last long weekend visit, five of Jod's very good friends have been diagnosed with breast cancer and one had a daughter die of alcohol poisoning her first week away at college. Old Tom Jod' has always been severe, but over this past year she has got herself stuck in an especially thick mire of doom and self-loathing. Two of those friends, Tannis and Gwendolyn, had breasts removed.

I should go ahead and chop off a titty, too, was all Jod' had to say when she heard. Or chop both'em off and donate them to Tannis and Gwen. A booby for each. Lord knows I'm not using mine.

With Jody and I it's not a matter of sex, not a matter of sexuality.

I love her and have in the past offered to please her. Early in our relationship I would try to kiss her breasts, but she would knock me away, telling me not to bother. She doesn't believe that her body was made to receive, let alone achieve, pleasure. With a joking self-deprecation has Jod' always declared this. Only now, seeing other women equipped perfectly for life being hurt, has the unfairness of her own lot taken a fatal chomp out of her. Jod' has always taken the poor hand she was dealt with brave and belligerent righteousness. She has suffered so the rest of us didn't have to. But now those who have always been gorgeous and fleet footed are getting theirs. And if Jod' cannot be the one that has it the worst, what good is she? Such is her thinking.

Night had fallen enough for the fireworks to start. With a whistle they were lobbed into the sky, cracking open with light. Each spidery blast illuminated the twins in flashes of blue and green, only to then become a silhouetted tangle of limbs and shouts in the darkness that followed. Those same outbursts elucidated Jod's gruesome, sloshed face as she watched the twins with dead eyes that had not so long ago beamed with ebullient disgust. Breasts aside, she won't even let me hug her anymore.

She raised her cup to me. From generations of washing the picture of Whinny the Pooh was completely faded

"So I guess happy Canada Day", she said, downing her drink. My husband I met when I was hired to photograph him for his dust jacket. He didn't want the hackneyed pretension of scribe before bookcases, or contemplative face looking elsewhere, drowned in moody shades. Instead, I suggested that I let myself into his apartment an hour before he usually woke up and wait by his bedside. When he was rousing I took his photo. Everyone thought that was just brilliant. After five years of marriage I came home early one afternoon in September to find six-year-old Beth with his penis in her hand. Without packing even a change of clothes I took her right then and drove the night from Corbet to the family cottage in North Bay.

For a few summers the cottage had gone unused, and had been mostly gutted in anticipation for major renovations that still haven't been made. That first day we made due with what had been left. Just a few sippy-cups and board games missing important pieces, all that lingered from years ago, from my own childhood spent here.

Nina, the twins' mother, is the same age as my daughter. She was a godsend for Beth, who had spent the winter and spring of '72 alone and confused with me in a summer cottage that didn't have a television.

There had been no divorce. After leaving, I never saw or spoke to my husband again and he never came after us. This spring, when I asked Jod' to marry me, she said she'd do it only if I called him up and demanded official walking papers. With a smack that cracked like a firework, I reddened Jod's cheek and she loosened my left canine. Old Tom Jod's a beast. But aren't we all.

Nina and Tim have always left the twins in our care whenever they wanted a moment's peace.

In all the years I've known her, the only time I have ever seen Jod' actually happy was when she would play with those two, tickling their soft white bellies or hauling them across beach like some ogre, one under each arm. She had tried to be that way with my daughter, but Beth, when she was little, was not so good with strangers. And now that she's older and now that Jod's become a more defined aspect of my life, Beth won't acknowledge her at all.

This weekend the twins were left with us while Nina and Tim went into town for party favours. No sooner had they pulled out of the gravel driveway did Eric gash open the bottom of his foot on a sharp rock in the lake. He kept screaming that he'd been bitten by a jellyfish. He would not believe Jod' when she assured him that there are no jellyfish in Lake Nipissing. The only way to quiet him was to play along.

Eric's face turned from vexed to befuddled as Jod' crouched over his foot and pulled aside the crotch of her one piece. His skin blanched as she relieved the sting, leaving him with a ghost-white face freckled by red petechia.

"Feel better?" Jod' asked, a genuine, dulcet hint to her voice, as she cupped his chin in a manner both fatherly and motherly.

Eric only nodded, dumbfounded, but assuaged nonetheless.

When Tim and Nina returned, the four of us were long gone to the hospital. Our rush had been such that we hadn't thought to leave a note.

Two hours later, when we returned with the twins, Nina, overly frazzled, informed me that our babysitting services would never again be needed. Jod' smashed the plate she was washing when I told her.

"That stupid bitch," she seethed. "Probably figured that the two old women with fish breath had up and snatched her darlings."

Their father came out onto the beach now. Erica waved at us as she was led into the house, but Tim brought his daughter's hand back to her side. Jod' took the top off her cup and drained it of its last drops.

"I can't say I love you, Barb. Maybe I do," she said. "Or maybe it's not that I love you, but just hate myself to much."

Her toes gripped into my stomach again like a frightened hand.

***

when we had stayed a full week at the cottage, Eric
photos of us on the beach with a disposable camera.
otographer made them want to be photographers
er they had the photos to show us first thing. At
market they were misdeveloped. The lab had printed the
negatives so our skin came out blue and our teeth black.

There is one deadpan photo of Jod' that I asked to keep. In the
photo she isn't smiling, but grimacing, hating having her picture
taken, hating having any attention brought to the fact that she is
corporeal, but doing it for the twins. She has all her hair in the
picture. Her face is as dark as usual and extra hateful, but, as it is
with negatives, her orifices beam. There is a great light and a great
energy that shines out from Jod's nostrils and mouth and eyes, a
powerful white energy that would explode and elucidate the whole
world were it not for being stymied by this scowling, black shell.

In negativity even there can be radiance sometimes.

Giving Up The Ghost

Please you, draw near

Ashley Inkpen had been draped over the couch, nursing a lazy little chub, when his mom rang from a hospital payphone to say that Becca had had an incident.

Ashley's sister had collapsed again, this time on stage during her *Tempest* dress-rehearsal. Her doctor couldn't say how serious, his mom relayed, but Becca had yet to regain consciousness. Mrs. Anderson from next door had been alerted and the old bat would be swooping by in just two shakes of a lamb's tail to pick him up.

Few and far between were the times Ashley ever had the run of the house, so the plan was to make a morning of it. With Becca at the Little Theatre—she was Miranda in the much anticipated production—and his mom sniffing out bargains at the Farmer's Market, he had pounced on the chance to strip. Ashley ate a bowl of cereal, hard, standing at the kitchen island like the sheriff of some small town, his nudity his pistol and his badge. Having made barely a dent in thirteen, wood had been creeping up on Ashley all summer long like the shivers and sweats of an illness, an illness for which there seemed to be no remedy. Pump, pull, beat and stroke, he could choke and tickle all the live-long day but could not cure his affliction. For this he blamed his sister.

Without the threat of being walked in on, he could get down to some serious, unabashed surgery. Getting comfy, he settled into the couch, took up the flicker, and found his way to the music station.

Samantha Fox! Hello nurse! On the TV set now, she lip-synched. That Limey tart! Punked-out and leather-clad, she swivelled saucily in shredded denim and beaten leather before her fake music video audience. Frayed tassels dangled at the corners of the ripped jeans. Surely one of them had to be some sort of lynchpin that, if tugged, would denude Sam entirely.

"Touch me. Touch me," Sam enjoined. The stage lights turned her peroxide-white locks yellow and pink. Her hair was a sea of sex-tousled waves. Oh, she'd been wrestling all right. "I want to feel your body. Your heartbeat next to mine."

She sang as if directly to him. The corduroy texture of the couch scratched his bare bottom tenderly, warm and ticklish. She sang—and so Ashley did Sam's work for her gladly. When he was not afforded the luxury of video, he would sometimes sneak into his sister's room to steal her tapes, listening with his Walkman in bed. Though Becca's collection consisted mostly of Talking Heads, Violent Femmes and the Clash, Ashley knew where to snoop for his sister's guilty pleasures, her Madonna, her Tiffany, her Samantha Fox.

Ashley might have gone the whole messy megillah that morning too, but for commercial breaks. A good pace, a decent rhythm and a sufficient divorce from reality were fundamental and were impossible to establish and maintain before the station had to pay its bills.

One channel above music videos was sports. He flicked to the highlights and softened slowly, bobbing like an old man fighting sleep in a shaft of afternoon parlour light. This was a little old man he had, after all. Ashley was his mother's son but for this wrinkled geriatric dangling between his bare thighs, a wise and wily old coot that cast him under all sorts of enchantments.

The highlights. Game five of the series tonight. Do or die. Sir David Stieb was starting on the hill against Oakland. An early-season interview with Kelly Gruber, the Toronto Blue Jay's third baseman, was playing. "He's a great pitcher," Kelly was saying of Stieb in his deadpan Texan drawl. "He's a competitor. He's a guy that we call a gamer as well. You know, when the chips are down, you want him in there because he's a fighter. He doesn't quit. He doesn't give up. That's the thing that keeps him going."

Ashley dug his finger in his bellybutton hollow, and considered Gruber's flaxen mullet. It spilled from beneath Gruber's cap and halted just before his broad, blue shoulders. He scooped around the cheese in there, and brought it up to his nose for a good long sniff.

After a season riddled by lows of torpor and highs of pluck, the so-called Come Back Kids seemed to be at the dogs' end now. The Jays were behind three games to one in the American League Championship Series and the overall feeling was that, against the Oakland Athletics, they didn't stand a chance. But then again, with Toronto you could never be sure. The Boys in Blue had come out of spring training in Dunedin as dark horses, a team to watch. After opening the season with six one-run games—four of which they lost—all of 1989 seemed shot to hell, no different than '88 or '87 or '86 for that matter. Toronto had some returning heavies—George Bell, Kelly Gruber, Fred McGriff and Tom "Henkenstein" Henke— okay, but even they seemed interned in this slump. All the right elements were in place for a great team, they just weren't coagulating.

Call the slump a growing pain, maybe. Born in '75—the same as the Jays' inception—Ashley could bitch a song or two about the aches that came with aging. His own body, like the thirteen-year-old club, was struggling with coordination. Their strides were lengthening, though their feet still tripped up. No wonder the bullpen was such garbage. Some nights they couldn't even hit the side of a barn, even from the inside.

Only when former batting coach Cito Gaston replaced Jimmy Williams mid-season did a sea change seem possible, if not imminent. That gentle looking man, quaintly moustachioed, must have stoked some great fire beneath his guys. In their dash they all of a sudden flourished. Their jib was altered, cut more precisely. Bats were finally finding balls and pitches reacquainted themselves with the strike zone. Play started to shape up all around. Then, in June,

Blue moved from Exhibition Stadium into the new
—the scrotum to the CN Tower's freestanding erection,
ter had pointed out—and hopes were gotten up sky high.
September, George Bell's twenty-two game hitting streak
arried the Jay's to first place, tied with the Baltimore Orioles.
In a movie-perfect climax, the two rival clubs played their last regular season games against each other. On September 29th—Showdown Series Weekend—a whole season of ebb and flow, failure and comeback, was distilled to three games. The Jays won the first when, on a wild pitch—with Gruber waving him in—Lawless stole home. 2 to 1 in the 11th inning. In game two, Henke closed 4 to 3, well into extra innings.

And so the American League East belonged to the Jays and all of Toronto erupted. All of Ontario and all of Canada lost their heads with jubilation. In the infield, the Jays piled into a writhing blue heap. A season's worth of steam blew off. There was bedlam in the streets of Toronto, traffic was jammed and horns blared long into the night. And all the while, choke as fiercely and as desperately as he did, Ashley came up clean and empty handed. Every bit of him seemed to gather in his wrinkled lower extremities, percolating but somehow unable to find the way out.

What made you hate and love the Blue Jays were their late-inning rallies. Just when you had cashed in your chips, were cursing and stomping your rally-cap into the dirt, they reached around and pulled from their behinds the most glorious horseshoes you'd ever seen.

Ashley couldn't bear to watch the debacle highlighted. As sure as he had been born, he was sure the Jays were done for. He felt it in his bones like the elderly sense storms. Tops in both offence and defence, the A's mowed through the Blue Boys effortlessly. The first two games at the Oakland Coliseum were the first two nails in the coffin. On home Astroturf the Jays won the third game and suddenly Toronto fans believed again. Game four, regardless of turf, went to Oakland and suddenly, again, ominous doom clouds hovered over the cityscape, presaging the end.

Built up all season, built up over three lousy years, the pressure was unbearable.

Just as the highlights showed Jose Canseco flex his triceps, ready to obliterate a Henke breaking ball, Ashley flipped a channel down and Sam came back to him in all her voluptuous constancy. Hello nurse! She was water instilled with healing salts. She was a therapeutic hot tub like the kind the Jays had in their new SkyDome locker room to sooth all aches. Some street tough now, mincing and dancing with other dancing street toughs, Sam assured Ashley that even naughty girls needed love too. Don't exempt the naughty ones. If anything, they need the most love. Man, did they ever.

Just as the blood rushed back to Ashley's lap, bringing back with it the fidgety blue ache, his mother phoned to say that Becca had had another seizure.

A few shakes later, the doorbell rang.

Now 'tis true I must be confined by you

Mrs. Anderson had no lips and her eyebrows were drawn in an arch of constant surprise. A sparse, hoary storm of hair curled over her head like an angry revelation. When the stark autumn sun rolled over the Oldsmobile's windshield, her storm became translucent, ghostly to the point that Ashley could see her bald pate through it. She was this *thing*, this corpse gussied-up in pearl broaches, thick wool skirts and thin blouses that showed off her bulky brassieres. She wore lipstick, but on top of nothing. She wore lipstick on top of skin. Skinstick is what she wore.

On the horn with his mom, Ashley had not disregarded the TV, had been unable to disregard the TV. She was on the deck of a yacht then, Sam, frolicking on the open water, which was sedate and shimmering green. The camera lingered on her crevices just long enough for Ashley to wonder if he had seen what he thought he had seen because he might not know what it was even if he saw it. The bawdy little codger he harboured assured him that yes, yes boy, that was what you thought it was, and sent Ashley into a frenzy. Terrible thing about his sister, really.

There had been no time to settle himself and now, with lipless, dusty Mrs. Anderson, doubled over the wheel, rushing to the hospital at 30 miles per hour, his chub was hemmed in between his jeans and his thigh, vibrating like a fly caught between two panes. To concentrate on the brittleness of Mrs. Anderson was doing no good. Thinking of how dry she was only made Ashley think of how dewy and soft Sam would be.

Lips must recede with age, he figured. Lips on young, beautiful people—lips on Sam Fox—seemed filled with juice, puffy, and inviting They were slick like an eyeball, had a sheen to them like they were so unbelievably alive. Oh boy.

"That sister of yours. She's a fighter," Mrs. Anderson mused, a tad tearfully. Her hands wrung the steering wheel. Blue snakes slithered over top of each other, blanketed beneath a thin sheet of liver spots. She was anxious about Becca, no doubt, and was stifling her emotions, putting on a decent face for Ashley's sake. Mrs. Anderson was one of the many friends, fans, and well-wishers of Corbet who had followed Becca's condition intimately, a support team rallying around her and pulling for her whenever waters got choppy. Living next door, having known Becca always, this must have been especially trying for Mrs. Anderson.

"Those doctors," she groused, "they keep predicting her time and she just keeps right on defying them. Always bounces back. A real fighter that one. So brave."

"I know. She is." It would be impolite to turn on the radio without asking. Even though Ashley was completely put out, he had been taught better manners.

"It's not easy."

"Yes. I know." he said. "It's not easy."

"To fight like that takes real strength. Real strength."

She stunk, that old bat. She reeked and she had the window rolled up, tight. Mrs. Anderson stunk to high heaven of a flowery perfume that was sharp, sharp like the barbs had been left on the stems. Overpowering was what it was, really, her perfume. Ashley's bellybutton lingered on his finger and he casually whiffed that.

"Yes. I know. Real strength." Ashley shifted uncomfortably in his seat, trying to adjust himself without adjusting himself, cursing his sister. Blaming her.

"When my husband was diagnosed with cancer the doctors gave him two choices."

"Yes."

"Yes. They gave Bob two choices. Either he could go untreated and live for a year, or he could do the chemo and maybe live for two." There were little hairs, wispy and white, showing through the red shellac of her skinstick. Her flesh was draped carelessly over her skeleton like a jacket on a chair back after a rotten day. "And old Bob, stubborn bum that he was, decided to fight. He fought tooth and nail, Bob. The radiation itself nearly killed him, forget the cancer. All that for a few extra months of life before he gave up the ghost for good. Now that's strength."

"Strength. Yes, I know." Ashley was sick. He was sick of hearing again and again about how strong his sister was. Becca wasn't strong. Sheesh. Manipulative was what she was. That's what he thought about the whole illness hullabaloo, though no one ever asked for his opinion.

And Bob Anderson hadn't been strong either. Ashley didn't say so, but he so wanted to—his manners. That old moribund had been home for two months before finally kicking the bucket. Out in the back yard, which was separated from the Inkpens' by a thin chain link, Bob Anderson would sit all day on his deck. Just a lump of skin, hair, liver spots, and Scottish wool, he would bake in the sun and tremor, looking at nothing. Gradually he would slump completely over and pass out into sleep. That life was nothing to fight for, as far as Ashley could discern from his own yard.

Chances were that her Bob was terrified to die, terrified like Mrs. Anderson was terrified. Already she was rotting and she knew it. Otherwise, why would she cover herself up like she did? Why all the make-up? Why the pungent perfume? All of it was a cloak over the decaying smell of her dying body. What's so strong, so brave, about shame? If Becca was really as strong as everybody claimed, then she wouldn't wear a wig after her surgeries. After they shaved her bald, why cover it up? If she was so strong?

Strong my eye, Ashley stewed. Bubbled, percolated.

In his anger he was clumsy and awkward, like wearing a pair of dress shoes bought two sizes too big with the idea that he would grow into them eventually. After all, he did love Mrs. Anderson, really, and had loved Mr. Anderson, loved the two of them like the grandma and grandpa he didn't have anymore. For that one month that his mother had taken a second job working evenings at Tim Horton's, the Andersons had watched over him and Becca. Ashley had sobbed torrents for Bob Anderson when he died and Mrs. Anderson's death would surely be emotionally rending when her time came, despite his hardening heart.

For distraction Ashley focused on the streets passing. Changed leaves, harvest yellow and rust red, were already being raked off front lawns and piled in front of the curb. Some still bagged their leaves. Halloween not too far away, some trash bags were Jack-o-lanterns. Some were even spiders, or lopsided skulls. The stark orange sun was getting heavy and low in the afternoon, ducking behind houses. When it shone it did so in bursts. Ashley winced at the shocks of light. His face flared in the window, fluttering with the shadows cast through the trees, before being drawn back entirely into the shade. Looking at his reflection, he could see right through it.

She was going on and on about seeing Becca perform *The Miracle Worker* years ago and just how talented she was. Mrs. Anderson was a season ticket's holder at the Little Theatre and was anxious to see her inhabit the role of Miranda. How apropos it was, she maundered, considering Becca's condition. How she imagined Becca as a beautiful innocent plagued by some mutated Caliban and how, with their magic, the doctors were a little like Prospero. "Aren't they?"

"And believe it or not," she continued dreamily, "I played Miranda in my time. Though that was in the mid-1940's. We had a man in black face for Caliban. It was a different time, you understand. But how I love that play." Mrs. Anderson straightened out of her hump and applied airs like lipstick. "'Nothing ill can inhabit such a temple. If the ill spirit has so good a hope, good things will, uh, strive to live in it.' Or something like that." She slouched back. "It was so long ago. It would be such a shame, though. For Becca not to play that role."

All of Ashley—arousal, wrath, and affection—was convening in his groin, like a late-inning infield pow-wow on the pitcher's mound.

"But, knowing your sister, she'll bounce right back. She always does." Like the deep fault lines on her face, there were chinks opening up in Mrs. Anderson's so-called strong front. Her voice was becoming uncertain and shaky, her lipless lips quivering. "She'll pull through and be ready for opening night I bet. She's that strong. It wouldn't surprise me. It really wouldn't."

Manners be damned, Ashley reached for the knob on the radio. A.M. for distraction. He found sports, but didn't want to hear about the Jays' inevitable loss that night. So he surfed the F.M. dial. Classical, then rock, then static. And from all that static she rose, throaty and randy. Sam Fox may have been a naughty girl, but, God, she still needed love like anyone else. Squall gathering, Ashley flicked the radio off and bit his lip, squirmed in the passenger seat, and cursed his sister.

This. This was strength, Mrs. Anderson.

Let me not ... dwell in this bare island by your spell
The initial storm had hit on the opening night of *Frankenstein* at the Corbet Little Theatre. Becca, seven years old then—when Ashley was only three—was playing the part of the cute little blonde girl murdered in the woods by that ugly monster reanimated. Even in such a small role, Becca had immediately become the cynosure of the local theatre community, a prodigy. Already the Little Theatre owners were atwitter from finally finding a young actress with chops broad enough to stage *The Miracle Worker* next season.

Sitting at the edge of the stage, with her little stocking legs dangling, Becca was merrily sniffing prop daisies. When approached by the trundling, mumbling Frankenstein's monster, Becca at first regarded him with over-the-shoulder indifference. Then she turned and horror swelled. The daisy drooped and the terror built gradually on her face in layers.

Last minute the director had decided that there was a certain something lacking in the scene. Intensity. No one blamed Becca— her performance was succinct, and riveting. Instead cast and crew alike agreed that the monster's performance was wanting. To kick up the intensity a few notches, to signify madness and violence, the director had added a strobe light. But there was no time to rehearse the addition before curtain.

Yowling in the monster's arms, Becca's eyes rolled back to show their glassy white bellies and her body began to twitch like a dog dreaming of squirrel chases. A clear rivulet of drool ran steadily from her mouth and pooled on the stage.

Epilepsy, the doctors had declared, so cocksure in the diagnosis. There was medication for that, so she popped those pills for a spell. And Becca was fixed until she collapsed again, vomiting, three years later during a gym class.

Pneumoencephalographic images were performed, perilously. The doctors drained all but a bit of the cerebrospinal fluid from around her brain and replaced it with helium, so that the X-rays would be clearer. And there it was, plain as the nose on her face. There was Becca Inkpen's tumour. A true tumour. A little white shadow on her dark brain, it was a primary fact of the rest of her and her family's life, a Grade 1 pilocytic astrocytoma. There, on her posterior fossa structures. Luckily it was benign. Thank heavens for that.

At ten Becca had her first craniotomy. The doctors opened up her skull and scooped her brain like a pumpkin. The initial resection failed though, and her next cavalcade of tests revealed that not only had the tumour come back but that it was now malignant. A second tag team attempt of resection and radiation was all for naught and, by the time she was thirteen, Becca Inkpen's benign Grade 1 pilo-cytic astrocytoma had flourished into a malignant Grade 4 astrocytoma, a glioblastoma multiforme. From then on her care was considered palliative and her life expectancy was truncated into two years. If she was lucky.

Ashley had had a huge and worried heart for his sister. Each time she left for the hospital, he prepared himself to never see her again. But always she returned. For months after he would sneak into her room while she slept. He would push aside the stuffed animals and climb aboard. To sleep, Becca would take off her wig, resting it on a Styrofoam bust on her dresser. Ashley liked his sister bald best. She looked futuristic with her shiny dome. Or she looked tough with a month's stubble—pink and hairless where the scars wended. Putting his cheek to hers, Ashley would fall back to sleep with the sound of her breathing, the sound of her surviving.

Always he would be woken up with a plush belly smothering his face. "Get the fuck out of my room, Little Turd," Becca would huff, shoving him off.

With so many people behind her, so many people pulling for her, it made no sense for her to die.

Tempest rehearsals began in late August. For two years though, the Little Theatre had been fundraising. This was to be the production to end all productions. Costumes were being rented from Stratford, and technicians brought in from Toronto. It was promised that the island set would be so lavish that the audience would be able to smell the dew sluicing off the real fronds. The opening storm would even employ rain machines and pyrotechnics.

The star of the show, Becca twirled around the house with her script rolled up in her fist. "Wherefor do I weep?" she asked her reflection in the microwave door, "At mine unworthiness, that dare not offer what I desire to give, and much less what I shall die to want." The curtain was not slated to go up until October 10th but she had been off-book since July.

Ashley was introduced to Sacha Deskar—Ferdinand to Becca's Miranda—the afternoon after the first cast meeting. He had been in the living room watching the Jays play a double-header against the Indians, when the two actors came in through the side door.

Sacha was twenty-one, four years older than Becca. He was a brawny ditz of a man, olive in skin tone. His jet black hair was buzzed on one side, and swooped into his eye on the other. Ashley shook hands with Sacha and watched as Becca led her leading man upstairs to her room. Probably they had to run lines.

Three up, three down, Sir David Stieb sent the Indians away swinging. Prone to late-inning hissie fits earlier in the season, Stieb was finally putting his head into the game, hitting his stride.

After about ten minutes Ashley heard the distant mumbles and dumb moans coming from upstairs. He had seen his sister seizure before and knew the telltale noises. Panicked, he took the steps two at a time to her room, where he found Miranda astride Ferdinand, ravishing him, bucking him angrily into the mattress.

Becca's curved back was to him, but Ashley could see Sacha's face, his head propped up on a pillow. He was wincing in pain. Becca leapt up and down, as if she was trying to leap clear off him but couldn't manage. She landed harder each time with a rough grind. Sacha grimaced and bore his teeth. Her blue bedspread was in a rumpled mess so it appeared to be a small, rectangular pool. Sacha was buoyant and Becca stayed afloat. The bunched and folded sheets gave the appearance of growing waves. She was sailing him some place.

"Wait!" Sacha howled. "Wait! Jesus! Becca! Becca! Okay! Stop! Quit! Fucking quit it!" Sacha tried to push her off but Becca only shoved him back and landed more vigorously. A cruel, wet sound slopped between them as well as a painful clacking of pelvic bones. The harder she rode, the more the sheets bunched, the higher the waves rose. Plush bears and cats floundered.

Becca's seizure became more furious and her howls more feral. Sacha quit his yelping. His bottom lip grew and began to quiver. His eyes frowned and moistened. Becca quaked, mumbled and shivered like a little girl mauled by monsters in a floriferous wood as she died all over Ferdinand.

Finished, she rolled off into the water, leaving her lover sore, his boat still afloat.

Becca did not shatter then, or the three other times Ashley had spied on her in her room with three different men. Watching her die this way, he felt duped to his fundament. So duped in fact, down right bamboozled, that he wanted nothing more than for her to up and die for real already. Torn, having no where else to turn, Ashley became a chronic masturbator, kowtowing and falling under the influence of his hard feelings and stiffening codger. Though he tried to pull this sickness out of him, nothing would yield, leaving Ashley lousy with a spirit that he didn't understand and couldn't exorcise.

The three times following her tryst with Sacha, Ashley had seen her with Doug Donaldson, Nick Johnson, and some blob of a man who he later found out was playing the ugly beast Caliban in the production. Hearing Becca's brink of death noises when their mom was away, Ashley would skulk daintily up to her room, wooed by this new hatred, shown the way by his divining rod. Through the sliver of view he peeped, longer and longer each time. There was a certain confusing joy he found in abhorring his sister. He couldn't not watch.

But release me from my bands with the help of your good hands
The Oldmobile ran around on the curb with a gruff scrape. Mrs. Anderson's sight was not what it used to be and certainly was not improved by the mists of grief worse than cataracts. Ashley slammed the door behind him. The old woman stayed there with the motor running, half on the curb and half on the road, her weak hands gripping the steering wheel.

Ashley leaned into the car. "Thank you for the ride," he said softly.

He loped into Corbet General, though in no rush to attend Becca. She'd be staying put. Ashley had other, more pressing matters to attend to: a washroom, lickety-split. The automatic doors knew not to get in his way. With a contorted, holding-it-in gait he moved past the flower and gift shop, past the pharmacy. In the lobby cans, reserved for the general public, he cussed the visible sneakers at the bottom of each stall door. An acrid wind filled his sails and he set his course. Out.

Through schools of waiting loved ones and the loved ill Ashley weaved in a pained, shark-eyed trance. Visitors sat in the chairs provided, reading and chatting amiably with one another or with random doctors and orderlies. Even after all the time spent in hospitals because of Becca, Ashley still found it weird how all those waiting for possibly life-rending reports managed to treat one another with the utmost civility.

He jiggled more knobs to no avail.

A dike of politeness held the flow of anxiety. Really, those waiting and those being waited on should have been blowing their tops with inchoate anticipation. They should have had a white knuckled grip of one another's lapels, ululating "Why? Why can't anyone tell me why?" or "When? When will they tell me what?"

In this hospital, a decade before, the truth of Becca's true tumour was issued, and Ashley's mother erupted with loud, wet sobs. Back-patting nurses led her away to some secret ward—the Hysterical Mother's Ward—so as not to disturb that diaphanous web of calm throughout the hospital. Ashley had stayed with Becca, a little six-year-old boy then. He lay with her on the slim examination bed, the brown paper crinkling beneath them. She had been so reserved then, detached, the only one to hold herself together. To most her attitude was a testament to the strength of her spirit, of her reluctance to give up. So it had seemed to Ashley too. In her strength he found his, until recently.

Now he meandered down the corridors with his bum stuck out and his groin tucked in, trying to obscure the tumescent rumpus in his jeans. There was a spot on his wrist where his watch usually was, where sweat would gather and fester. He let his nose stroke over and around that spot and was a little soothed.

Sniffing, not looking where he was going, Ashley collided with a lanky man wearing an eye patch. "Watch it!" the Cyclops grumbled, gripping onto Ashley's shoulder to keep himself from going down. Ashley held onto the man's elbow, briefly shocked out of his trance. As he looked into that mean old mug, into that one angry eye, he felt a long blue streak of swears fostering. To get them all out he would have to unhinge his jaw. Ashley wanted nothing more than to cover this pirate in frigs and fricks and other expletives that he thought but never spoke aloud, spewing curses until the man was dripping.

"Excuse me," Ashley murmured before moving on.

A TV in the patient's lounge on the rehabilitation ward was showing Oakland's star Ricky Henderson sliding, in slow motion, into second base, just under Nelson Lariano's tag. Henderson burgled the infield like a crooked employee of a home-security company. The cocksure runt moved like water, diving always onto his belly like Slip and Slide, and swooping back up into a stand flawlessly. At least Sir David was starting on the hill that evening. As long as Henderson was shut-out—McGuire and Canseco for that matter—the Jays might have a fighting chance. All the same, Ashley looked away from the set and kept waddling, ducking in and out of chronically occupied washrooms like some desperate fiend.

Enslaved was how he felt, helpless. Ashley was at the mercy of that old conjuror of dirty notions between his legs.

Other fans, seeing his jersey and hat, held up crossed fingers and shook their heads uncertainly. They all hoped the Jays would pull through. Have strength, they all seemed to say. We're all pulling. We'll pull through.

None of the receptionists stymied Ashley's crusade as he lumbered into the restricted wards. In his awkward position and harried look they must have mistaken him for a patient. A rare bone disease with a dash of schizophrenia maybe. Add to that his jersey and cap, he had the appearance of a terminal Make-A-Wish boy whose life was riding on the Jays winning that night.

Occupied stall after occupied stall, he eventually found himself in what appeared to be the Convalescence Ward, a floor below where Becca and his mom were, in Palliative Care. Patients skipped carefully on crutches, rolled jerkily in wheelchairs, or doddered in plaid slippers. They were doped and mellow, on the mend and smiling like goofs. He did his best to avoid another collision. In front of the first open door he found Ashley stopped and nosed in cautiously.

Hello nurse!

Boy oh boy, even in her papery uniform, smattered in a clunky mix of pastel strokes and dashes, she was something else. She was a waterbed out of the blue. The nurse had a broad, symmetrical face hardly muddied by products or lines and her hair, hay blonde, was bobbed just above her shoulders. She was a spitting image of Sam Fox but also bore a slight resemblance to Toronto Blue Jays third baseman Kelly Gruber, both of whom had flowing golden hair.

Like the mist that dallies above rapids, the nurse stood at the bedside of a cadaverous old man. Bushy and expressive, her patient had the white eyebrows of a retired illusionist and the flat, wide nose of a newborn. She set aside the blanket and lifted up the old man's gown. Sheesh. His penis lounged purple and wrinkled, about the stubby size of a big toe, in the mess of his hairy thighs. From the tip snaked a thin tube like a strand of spaghetti, connected to a heavy bag of urine dangling bedside. Ashley frowned to see the ugly thing and was about ready to resume his search when she took up the slack. The nurse asked the man if he was ready and he nodded uncertainly that he was. Gently, she began to tug on the catheter. His bit lifted to a sluggish attention and his eyebrows rose up to the middle of his forehead. The dead tensed back to life.

Unsullied by veins, the nurse's hands were soft and white, her wrists thin and delicate. With his bum out behind him, Ashley carefully spied as she reeled in her line from the dark waters of the old man's insides. He sniffed his wrist conspicuously. Cordoned off behind a drawn curtain there was another patient in the room. Gradually he was building up a momentum of a dry coughing fit which the nurse, set to her task, ignored.

Coming and coming, there didn't seem to be an end to the catheter. It kept revealing itself like a rainbow handkerchief from a magician's breast pocket. Ashley wondered how far it could be inside of the man. Gritting his teeth, the old man tried to muffle his discomfort. On the nurse's face was a look of apologetic concentration. She bit her bottom lip—seductively coy almost—in sympathy with his unease. Methodically being brought in, the line didn't stop, like a thread of life, some tangled essence that was being drawn out of every nook and cranny of the man by this nurse. Fitting then, that when the end finally did appear, dropping out dully, the old magician slackened and fell back onto his starched pillow with a sigh. He had a look of sheer elation on his face and seemed to fall dead asleep. She had helped him to die, maybe, untangling the anguished life knotted up and so sick inside.

Ashley's sails luffed.

Gentle breath of yours my sails must fill, or else my project fails, which was to please.

Sir David Stieb, number 37, had a no-nonsense moustache and a gruff frown. But as he leaned in to inspect the signs between Ernie Witt's thighs, you could see, even through his scrutinizing squint, that Stieb had kind, generous eyes. Witt would waggle his index finger, alone and small like some tiny dink, and Stieb would nod, accepting the sign for a fastball. Out of his stance, he would lean back on the mound, lift his knee into his armpit and lurch forward, as if falling. Then release, stretching his body at the last minute like a galloping horse. Stieb could strike out batters before they even finished tapping the red clay from their cleats. Mustard and stamina were his staples, though he was also notorious for choking under pressure and throwing tantrums. In a pinch, Stieb would often rant and rave himself back into his senses. An odd drama to watch, Stieb alone, out there on his mound self-conferencing. On his best day Stieb was that rare sort of pitcher—right up on the highest hill with Nolan Ryan and his cannon of an arm—who could sometimes finish a game he had started.

No-hitters are uncommon. In major league baseball's history, less than three hundred had been thrown. Incredibly rare—under twenty having ever occurred—are perfect games, wherein the pitcher doesn't allow a single hit. The infield can do all the work for a no-hitter, but a perfect game is all on the pitcher.

With two out in the top of the ninth, September 24, 1988, Dave Stieb was one out away from being the first Blue Jay to ever throw a no-hitter. The Cleveland Indian's Julio Franco pulled a piddly little double and the Jays won anyhow. Only a week later, facing the Orioles, Stieb, again, was one out shy of a no-hitter when Jim Traber got a grounder past Fred McGriff on first. Each time the Jays won, but still.

Then, the night of August 4, 1989, Stieb had struck out every New York Yankee in the line-up. X posters hung over the wall by the left field foul line, tallying his strike-outs, not moving at all in the stale summer air. After two curtailed no-hitters, Stieb was now one out away from slaying baseball's white whale, the ever elusive perfect game. Two down in the ninth, one out to go, Roberto Kelly, an unremarkable Panamanian by all standards, stepped into the batter's box. Kelly had barely touched the ball lately. A perfect game was as certain as death. Getting behind in the count with two pitches just outside, Stieb calmed and readied himself to finish. Knock wood. The fair-sized crowd gnashed their teeth, waiting to let loose the anxiety they had been storing since about the third inning, when Stieb had set his course.

Gnashed teeth became agape mouths when Stieb gave up a single to left stretched into a double. That was all it took. Stieb had been feeding Kelly breaking balls, when he should have been shaking Witt off until he got the go for a fast ball. He was, for the third time in two years—having come closer than the majority of pitchers will ever come—robbed blind. Though he kept his cool, Stieb's perturbation came out in the nervous adjustment of his hat, the grave-deep groove he dug in front of his rubber and the incessant crotch adjustments.

The crowd waited politely for the end of a game they no longer cared about.

He burrowed his chin into his chest and pulled down the brim of his hat to hide his eyes from the now wilting crowd. With his head down he gathered himself back together. And when his head snapped back up he settled into a stance as fresh as the first inning.

Stieb struck out the next batter and the Jays beat the Yankees easy as pie. He walked off the mound technically victorious, having closed a game he had started. Though, in the new terms he had set for that game—in the eyes of the let down fans, and surely in his own—he walked away a loser.

Now my charms are all o'erthrown, and what strength I have's mine own, which is most faint.

A few doors down from where the nurse was now ravelling the catheter like an extension chord, Ashley barged into an empty private room. The bed was made and the spread smoothed out, waiting. On the bedside table was a vase of lilacs and above the bed a tacky, bulk painting of flowers also in a vase. Tied to the bed frame was a cluster of swollen balloons, with GET WELL SOON written on them, no doubt waiting for a well-to-do youngster just relieved of his tonsils.

The commode was small, periwinkle and smelt of chlorine.

Collapsing on the seat in a rush, Ashley fumbled with his belt and took down his pants. Sam Fox came to Ashley warmly like the tide, lapping at his ankles. The suds from her breakers lingered as a fizz on the faint hair on his legs. This was a languid, familiar love. Her salty tide was flowing. Oh nurse! Sam's waters gripped at the shore quicker now, rising above his knees and then to his waist, eventually swallowing Ashley up to his neck and taking him out to her wide open sea. The fervour with which he handled himself was uncertain, belonging to that ambiguous rendezvous of desperation and desire. Either way, he was hardly gentle. The waters, too, grew choppy. The waves rose and stabbed in his nose. A yellow lather formed and as the storm gathered momentum, Sam began to blur and meld with the image of Catheter Nurse, which was fine by him. There were a few different currents whorling. Though he was now taking whatever he was given, Ashley could work with that. After all, this was a hybrid of hotness, with a look of understanding, of sympathy for Ashley's condition. Regardless of vitriolic notions she would care for him tenderly. Slowly she reached out and began to remove from him the thin thread of life he imagined was wadded up inside. In his guts there was a sickly twinge, tangled as they were like Christmas lights. Then. A swell of dizziness gathered in his head like the mucus of flu, clouding the pictures he was trying to conjure. Momentarily, his head was dunked. When he came up, his eyes were blurry with salt sting.

Ashley kept a pace and tried to organize his fantasy, tried to keep his head in the game. Behind the gathering fog it was hard to discern the difference between Sam, the nurse and—was that maybe Kelly Gruber, crouched at third, glove in the dirt, ready, like a parent waiting with open arms to receive a first-stepping toddler? He tried to reorganize the confused parts of this motley monster he was unwittingly creating, attempted to appease these waters. Ashley adjusted his Jays cap a few times and stayed the course.

Thunder moaned. Or maybe that had been Ashley that made that noise. Apparently shocked, his legs were overcome by paroxysm. His stomach seized and his toes curled until that mess of pictures and sounds was swept away entirely by the rush of the surf, foaming white and rolling over him, sousing him good.

On the pot, Ashley swooned as if he had stood up too quickly. Maybe a seasick nausea. Nothing then, a silence as if he had succumbed to the waters.

A few hot splashes hit his calf and dampened his sock.

Breaching, Ashley felt anonymous and groggy, unsure who or where he was. Washed back up on solid shore, he was drained and tired. When finally he did open his eyes he was half expecting, sort of hoping, to find the walls and bathroom door lavished and dripping with his bilious spirit, with all the illness, ire and desire that had been hectoring him for months. A filthy, noxious mess to justify the filth and mess he had been feeling all that time. Or maybe some slick and pungent tangle of yarn. Instead there was only a viscous slug's trail along his knuckles, a couple pathetic dashes on the back of his leg and dark spots like raindrops or tears smattering the underwear bunched at his ankles.

He poked at his rheumy end curiously. Once so powerful, it

was wrinkled and withered now like fast ball sign shaken off. Holding his sullied hand to his nose he took a smell. It smelt like nothing, nothing interesting at least.

And my ending is despair unless I be relieved by prayer, which pierces so that it assaults mercy itself and frees all faults.

That night, October 8, 1989, the Toronto Blue Jays hosted the Oakland Athletics at the SkyDome for game five of the American League Championships. The Dome spilled over with Jays' fans frantically waving white team scarves above their heads in support. Seen from above, the wave of fifty thousand in attendance roared and rolled, nothing held back.

By the seventh inning, the Athletics were four runs up and the few remaining scarves that twirled seemed to do so in surrender now. Giving up hits and stamina waning, Gaston got on the horn to the bullpen and pulled Stieb, putting Jim Acker in.

In the eighth a Lloyd Moseby homer put the Jays on the board and in the bottom of the ninth George Bell knocked one far out into the stands. Tony Fernandez hit a single to centre and then stole second. Ernie Witt grounded out but Fernandez took third. A sacrifice fly from Kelly Gruber brought Fernandez home and now the Toronto crowd was on their feet again, revivified by this familiar comeback scenario, scarves twirling like a stripper's undies.

Junior Felix stepped up to the plate and it seemed perfect. Felix wasn't a homerun hitter, but he was a consistent batter. If he got on base, then Lariano after him, Mosbey, who had already homered once, might at least bring one or both of them in to tie if not win.

Dennis Eckersley struck out Felix and the Athletics won the series. Close but no cigar. The A's advanced and would play the San Francisco Giants in the World Series. Cars were turned over in Oakland that night while, in Toronto, residents slumped home and out-of-towners sat solemnly with their families in a 401 jam.

His sister still not having regained consciousness, Ashley snuck away that night to watch the loss in one of the general waiting rooms. And, though he hated both teams and was forced by his mom to stay by Becca, Ashley would sneak away whenever he could to watch the World Series. The little boy in him still doted on the game, watched with a rapt, ebullient vacancy, while his burgeoning coldness towards his sister had him squirming to get as far away from her bedside as possible. What his mom was holding on to he couldn't figure. Becca would not live much longer, that was certain. Death was imminent and a round the clock vigil struck him as a waste of time. When there wasn't a game on he would watch music videos. And when his mom was off getting fresh coffee from the cafeteria, Ashley would unravel his tangled nerves in his sister's private washroom, becoming an old hand in no time at all, a skilled conjuror himself.

Becca resurfaced in the early hours of October 17, changed. States altered, she cursed and growled now as if possessed by some devil.

"As a matter of fact," her doctor mused, "actions that had once been attributed to demonic possession in the past were most likely the result of brain tumours." He was smooth and completely hairless, the doctor, not even having eyebrows. He looked like a fanatical swimmer or maybe a seal. "But we know better now."

In sharing this, the doctor's eyes sparkled with professional fascination. Miss Inkpen's disquieted glare had him avert his enthusiasm to the ground and stop mid-sentence. Becca swore and spat and dared everyone to go right ahead and fuck her. She burned her eyes directly into Ashley's. "Fuck me, Turd!"

Becca's doctor did his best to comfort the bewildered Inkpens, assuring them that modified behaviour, usually acerbic and peculiar, was par for the course. She didn't mean what she was saying and, to a degree, was legitimately haunted, if they chose to view her tumour as some torturous fiend. She had probably always been affected, as a matter of fact, though the effects in the past months and years leading up to this day may have been more subtle. Any character changes caused by the tumour would most likely have been tangled up with the mood alterations of puberty.

Hearing this diagnosis, Ashley's immovable opinion of Becca

gave, though just slightly. Over and over he replayed each of her raunchy displays, tossing this new excuse at each one to see what would stick and what would eek slowly to the ground.

In her thrashings, Becca threw her bedspread into a tizzy, raising her own waves and splashing in them, panicking in them and drowning in them. Her cheeks were flushed and her blonde curlicues knotted and tangled. Both Ashley and his mom kept a terrified distance from Becca at first, cautious of being scratched or punched, but her doctor encouraged them to not be afraid, to comfort her, to touch her all the same. Having her feet held calmed Becca's fight, though not her cursing. Soon, Miss Inkpen was brave enough to sit with her, petting her hair. Ashley kept at the other end of the room, in a chair beneath the TV, his leg spastic and his nails bitten. He wasn't so much frightened by his sister, but immobilized rather by the sheer largeness of the rancour that he had been able to feel for her just days earlier.

Later that evening, while Becca slept sedated, the Loma Prieta earthquake struck the Bay Area via the San Andreas Fault and was felt by the fans in attendance at Candlestick Park, where the third game of the World Series was to be played. Ashley sat in the waiting room, watching the news report. The tremor had rolled through the stadium like a weak but noticeable wave. Lights swayed and concrete shivered. After the quake passed, fans, restless in their anticipation, began to manically chant, "Play ball! Play ball!" unaware that 66 had died and 3,757 had been injured. A slew more would have died surely, as the earthquake hit during rush hour and had collapsed Cypress Street Viaduct on Interstate 880. As it happened, so many had ducked out from work early to catch the game.

A cerebral edema did Becca in, taking five days to finish her off. Chinks opened in her blood-brain barrier and water began to well. She continued to rant and rave, though when she lost her eyesight she mellowed considerably. During the last two days of her life she was swaddled completely by hallucinations and psychotic episodes. By then, while still insisting at keeping with her, Miss Inkpen had let go of her hope. Once jittery, her eyes now abated, slouching from weariness. After bouncing back countless times, proving everyone wrong, defying death, Becca had kowtowed irrevocably. Miss Inkpen attended her daughter with sorrowful torpor, waiting out the inevitable. Worry lines aged her. They aged Ashley too.

When he would glance over to his mom she would be watching him, not Becca. Her parents, husband and now her daughter— Ashley was all there was. She feigned a tight smile, reassurance that everything would be good again some day surely. She would pat and squeeze his shaking knee, her eyes dolorous and heavy. Together they waited, bored.

Mrs. Anderson stopped by twice, to see how things were coming along. She brought pie and tarts and told Ashley that he had to be strong, for his mom, for his sister, and for himself. He allowed himself to be calmed by the lipless kiss she put on top of his head and inhaled her barbed potpourri.

Out of respect, *The Tempest* never was performed on the Corbet Little Theater's stage. However, it did debut in Room 3 of Corbet General's Palliative Care Unit. The elaborate set and entire cast of sailors, spirits and monsters were present only in Becca's frazzled head. Miranda's lines were all that was audible to Ashley and his mother, and they came in fits.

"Do you love me?" Miranda asked one night, surprising her brother and mom out of catnaps. Though Becca was blind, her head rolled on the pillow to gaze vacantly at Ashley as if addressing him. The room waited as her imagined Ferdinand delivered his line in Becca's ether, telling her that he did indeed.

And Ashley, of his own stormy conscience, bowed his head and answered softly to himself that yes, he did, after all.

"I am fool," Becca then gushed, "to weep at what I am glad of."

"What is't?" she cried suddenly after an hour of rest. "A spirit? Lord, how it looks about! Believe me, sir, it carries a brave form. But 'tis a spirit."

Even as her ghost was going from her, Becca continued her

performance. No doubt she would have been marvellous in the role, at once playing Miranda's naïve innocence and the devious curiosity of her youth.

The last lines Becca delivered before the gauze of a coma enveloped her entirely were Miranda's first. She beseeched up to the ceiling, up to nothing in her blindness. "If by your art," her voice faltered as her reverence for Prospero clashed with her confusion over his destructive magic. "If by your art, my dearest father, you put the wild waters in this roar, allay them. The sky, it seems, would pour down stinking pitch but that the sea, mounting to th' welkin's cheek, dashes the fire out. O, I have suffered with those that I saw suffer! A brave vessel (Who had no doubt some noble creature in her) dashed all to pieces!"

One tear of lingering poison snuck out and on to Ashley's cheek. Overwhelmed, he cried a clean, auspicious gale for his fled sister. In the weeks following, he shrunk away to almost nothing at all.

As you from crimes would pardoned be, let your indulgence set me free

On September 2, 1990, less than a year later after Becca Inkpen's death, Dave Stieb threw a no-hitter against the Cleveland Indians. In 1992, the Jays met Oakland again but this time won the ALCS four games to two. The SkyDome erupted volcanically. The Toronto Blue Jays, the so-called Comeback Kids, went on to win back-to-back World Series.

Make It a Better Place

"Coming together for just a second, a peek, a guess at the
wholeness that's way too big."

–*Political Song For Michael Jackson To Sing*, Minutemen

"Annish," I said. "ish shafe."

She tilted the rear-view mirror. In there I could see her eyes
made large behind her fishbowl glasses, so Janice must have been
able to see mine. In this way she stared at me, flickering her eyes
back to the road every so often. Probably "The Man in the Mirror"
played on her tape deck. His whole corpus was there in the passenger
seat, scattered among the directions Janice had printed off the
internet. Thirty or so years of rock solid, funky hits. Just under
three thousand miles of road. Her eyes goggled with panic, darting
to the road, darting to me. They were the eyes of a mother in a
crowded shopping mall who has just realized that her little boy is
no longer at her hip. A worried driver, Janice.

Between London and Sarnia, the 401 had been puckered into
two tight construction lanes and we were stuck trailing a garbage
truck hauling trash from Toronto to Detroit. Stretched out along
the backseat because of my cast, my head was resting against the
window and I could see the other lane clear as day. Oncoming traffic
was sparse enough, I could see. It was safe to pass.

"There'sh othing oming." My top and bottom lip scraped
together like two dry husks of a dead beetle as I tried to enunciate.

"Better safe than sorry," Janice said finally, readjusting the
mirror and seeming to ease off the gas a touch.

The big wheels in front of us chewed up the construction pebbles and spat them back at our windshield like cherry pits. Our speed—already cut from 100 to 80 km by the construction any way—was turtled even worse on account of the truck. At the rate we were going, my stepmother's saviour would be long crucified—would be long imprisoned and stretched wide in the showers by some hairy monkey named Bubbles—before we even penetrated the desert.

I closed my eyes and crawled back into my soggy hangover.

With maxillomandibular fixation you've got to watch you don't drown in your own bile. If I were to start yakking, the slim gap between my top and bottom teeth wouldn't be wide enough to let everything through. The denser bits would get caught in the crisscrossing wires holding my jaw in place, eventually damming any passage. So back down into my lungs that puke would go. In case just such an emergency arose, my doctor in Montreal had equipped me with a handy pair of wire cutters. Only, Janice had been in such a rush to leave for California that she forgot to pack these for me.

Since I'd polished off the month's supply of hospital-issued liquid codeine my first weekend home, there had been little else to help pass the time. I put out a call to my older brother, and he delivered. Greg had sat with me on my bed, taking a few Jager swigs himself while he itched under my cast with a bent out coat hanger. When I'd seen him last—that must have been the summer before I left for McGill—he had been thirty-eight and not so different from the way he had been at twenty-eight, still wearing t-shirts that were too tight for him and glasses that he didn't need. Forty all of a sudden, newly wed to a palaeontologist named Anna and no longer wearing collared shirts and ties tongue-in-cheekly, he seemed finally old to me. Or maybe it was just being confined to the bed I had first masturbated in, being nursed and coddled by Janice and subsisting on bland slurries, soups, and pabulums, maybe it was all that that made me feel particularly young. And, just as he had when I was little, Greg had been the one that had to hook me up. Only it was different now.

"You've really fucked things up this time, Will," was about all Greg had to say to me, was all I remember him saying before I passed out. In my vacant stomach, the deer head had charged full tilt, antlers down.

Of course, the threat of drowning is paradoxically lessened because, with my jaw sealed, it's been nearly a month since I've actually eaten.

At the border the sun was setting in a callow sort of way. The sky over the U.S. was a thin wash of yellow with a few rose clouds streaking across like cat scratches on allergic skin. We had finally lost the dump truck, but damage enough had been done. Four stones had hit to do significant harm. Four points of impact shimmered in the dusk, each with a few spider legs searching out across the windshield to grasp tips with each other.

In her tapes, Janice was in mid-'80s for the second time now, a decade when major disagreements between street gangs could be settled through elaborate, impromptu dance routines. Or so I gather. Solos, pairs, and the out and out rumbles of pirouettes, back flips, and headstands. Times certainly have changed. As times will do. Or maybe it's only our willingness to accept such notions that has changed. Changed for some of us. Others, like Janice and like the rest of them flocking to the justice centre, ardently prefer to live in the past.

Slowing to the customs booth, Janice lowered the volume on the stereo. A bulky Muppet with a bristly push-broom moustache, the boarder guard looked up lazily and into our car. Janice stretched out our passports to him as though she was reaching for fast food.

"Where're you folks coming from?" the guard asked, studying our information and chewing the corners of his moustache.

"Ontario," Janice said clearly, militarily. "Corbet."

"Mhm. And where're you all guys headed?"

"California. Santa Maria."

"And what's you business there?"

The guard reacted to Janice's response in about the same way I had. Amused incredulity. And his face fell a second time when he saw me in back: two blotchy, blue commas under my eyes, punctuating a mushy, swollen nose and jowls puffed out and yellow.

"Welp," he said, handing back our bundle of proof apprehensively. "Good luck with *that*." He waved a finger back at me. "Myself, I hope they hang that weird little pervert. Have a safe drive now, Mrs. Fagel. Kid."

Before Janice had a chance to muster a comeback, the guard had shut his window and let up the blocker for us to pass.

With both hands firmly at ten and two, Janice stayed put. Her hackles rose. Should she reach out and tap politely—maybe violently—on the guard's little plastic window and, as her lather built, preach to and castigate him until he understood? I mean, really understood. Truly understood. But what could she say? She didn't even seem to really, truly, or fully understand the reasons behind the trip. The pilgrimage. Only that it was something that she had to do, something that I had to be there for. Cracks spread across the windshield of her purview, nearly meeting to the points where cracks become breaks.

The sun was setting, the music hummed, and Janice idled, trying to muster the brass.

Except Janice has always been light in the brass department. It was meekly even that she entered my family. Apologetically that she became my mother. "You don't have to call me 'Mom' if you don't want to" were her first words to me as my legal guardian. And then, as an afterthought, as a footnote, she added, "Though I'd very much like you to want to. Someday maybe. There's no rush." Maybe if she had insisted. If only. But, as Janice likes to say: If if's and and's were pots and pans, there would be no need for tinkers.

So she stayed with her arms constantly open, ready for me to run into her bosom at any moment, mewling "Mommy, Mommy, I need you." Two months after she adopted me, my 74-year-old father, her new husband, collapsed on an indoor tennis court. As time has gone on it's as if her open arms have tired and fallen to her sides, leaving Janice shrugging, pleading. Instead of saying Please, Please, she was now whimpering When? When?

"Anneish!" I coughed, elbowing the back of her seat.

Just as the border guard was opening his window to shoo us along, Janice put the car back into drive and moved ahead slowly, slinking shamefully into Michigan. Turning the tunes back up, tuning into better times.

As far as accidents go, man, I'd eaten it like a toddler into a bowl of chocolate ice cream.

If you've never had it happen to you, being hit by a pigeon is a little like being walloped by a dirty old sock filled with dust bunnies and dirt clods. A surprisingly heavy and thick filthy old sock.

Off balance, I turned my front wheel directly into one of the more cavernous potholes that hug the curb along Rue Sherbrooke. I would have flown clear over my handlebars were it not for my shoes' unwillingness to unclip themselves from the pedal clips.

To see this in slow-mo would be amazing. See, here's me bucking, doing a backwards pop-a-wheelie. If we can zoom in here, you'll notice that, because my wheel turned suddenly from the spin, so did my handlebars, to which were of course attached my hands. See that? And it's because my arms are crossed over one another—momentarily tangled and locked like a prisoner waiting to be shackled—that I wasn't able to put anything between my face and the bumper of the car parked in front of that Corolla.

If not for my chin hitting the bumper first you can see that my nose would have been staved into my brain. Lucky, that.

Complete mandibular fracture, nasal fracture, and tibial and fibulal fractures. Blood flowed over my face in thin, fluid strands like hair on a blustery day. The pain was so immense that it didn't register, was just one giant bellow of hurt that became so loud as to become no sound at all.

To be frank about it, that afternoon I did eat a pizza garnished with about half a gram of mushrooms, which probably had a hand in obscuring the hurt. Yet I was crippled to such an extent that, even if it was my traffic negligence that had caused the accident, I was clearly the victim.

Except for my backpack, which—as the first cop to arrive on the scene discovered as he searched for my ID, seeing as I was helpless to pronounce my name—contained roughly four pounds of ganja grown in the darkest, most fecund basements of the Calgary suburbs, doled out into different sizes of Ziploc baggies for our customers' convenience.

Despite spending my last year of high school up to my neck in a hardening mud bath of ketamine, I graduated an Ontario Scholar and, riding inheritance, was accepted without fuss to McGill. Some guys that I had met in an English Lit survey were involved in a door-to-door pot delivery service. Ding Bong, it was called. Like a doorbell: ding-dong. The owners, Mookie and Caleb, they were big into Captain Beefheart and definitely not marketing wizards, but they would get me high for chump change or else for free and they gave me a job. When pressured by the police I didn't bat an eye giving them up.

Instead of a jail sentence and a criminal record, I left Montreal with a fine. I wasn't so worried about my knob-job employers. Social excommunication was about the worst they could do to me. Besides, I was confident that they'd probably be thrown a bone too. As near as I could tell, the police were more interested in the possible affiliations between their rinky-dink pot service and an up-and-coming biker group from Hamilton testing waters in Montreal.

As soon I was able to move, Janice packed me into the back of the Civic—much like we were a month later, on our way to Santa Maria—and secreted me back to Corbet, where she relished mothering me back into the pink. During that whole drive and the weeks following I waited for an eruption, for some reprimand. At the very least a weepy lamentation. But there was only quiet. I'm sure that, more than anything, Janice was stifling elation at finally having me where she wanted me: as incapable and needy as a little baby.

My childhood bedroom became my convalescence room. In no uncertain terms I had informed Janice that, once I was gone, I would be gone for keeps. So she went and turned my old room into a guestroom. Sort of. She painted over my once maroon walls with a navy blue and added a trim around the ceiling with knobby nautical steering wheels on it. Where I once had a poster of Frank Zappa naked on the toilet there was now a very pedestrian painting of a schooner at sea. Other than that one painting, the walls, dresser, and bedside table were covered with photos of me, all before the age of eleven. My hair cowlicked, my cheeks chubby with glee and baby fat. Teeth precariously missing, food on my face. Funny that I have greedy-squirrel cheeks again, and teeth missing. Bruises around my mouth like a meal.

A good thing that I had my wire cutters handy the first time I saw what she'd done.

Biliously. Biliously masturbated by the pop star. Or, ceremoniously. The boy was ceremoniously masturbated by the pop star. Or unceremoniously, for that matter. How about frivolously? Caustically, then. Petulantly, maybe. Willfully.

That's how the driving game I invented went.

By midnight on the first day of the pilgrimage, heading West towards Wisconsin, the I-80 was dark and carless. The luminescent boards of direction flared green when we came within fifty-or-so feet and shone back at us, casting a sickly tinge in the car for a moment until we passed and fell back into the muted yellow of the stooping interstate lights.

I hadn't been out of bed more than twelve hours, but was dozy anyway with this lolling lethargy, where I'd slip into and out of lucidity. Most of my nausea had by then passed, but in its place had flared an irascible itch. Along with wire cutters, Janice had also left behind the coat hanger I had been using to reach the impossible agitations beneath my cast. About an inch above my ankle, a tickle that became a shiver, which swelled to what felt like a whorling, gradual paralysis. Rot down there, it felt like, sneaking up my body with its thorny tendrils.

It got so irritating that I was able to discern its shape. The itch was a small, biting rectangle that was bulky and may as well have had a pulse. My leg vibrated like a hive, keeping me awake. So I played this car game with myself to pass the time. A game to draw my attention from the itch that was fanning out like the cracks in our windshield.

Complacently. Derisively. Foolishly. Timidly.

The boy was altruistically masturbated by the pop star.

The odd transport would trundle up beside us, startling Janice. I was no good to drive, what with my cast and all. And anyway she was hell-bent on going the whole way to California without sleep. That's about twenty-six hundred miles. About forty hours straight. Every time she drifted into the lane next to her the warning bumps grumbled angrily beneath us, rumbling the whole car, keeping us both from sleeping.

In his oeuvre I believe Jackson goes from Bad to Dangerous. From Bad to Dangerous to Pedophilic.

Succinctly. Sacrosanctly. Meaningfully. Mendaciously. Critically. Gently.

"Boy Gently Masturbated by Pop Star" read a newspaper headline I saw earlier this summer. Or something to that tune. Maybe the pop star had been gently masturbated by the boy. I don't recall who gently masturbated who exactly. What stuck with me and struck me as immensely funny and gradually more repugnant (and then really funny again) was the need to qualify the quality and type of masturbation that had occurred. The Accuser—thirteen-year-old Gavin Somebody—was at one point uproariously masturbated by the pop star. The Minor was serendipitously masturbated by the pop star. The Cancer Boy was quixotically masturbated by the pop star.

The itch was like a ticking clock when you're baked. If you pay it the slightest bit of attention you'll become transfixed to the point where you begin to lose your shit in a very serious way. The adverbs were a soothing ointment. A calamine lotion.

Crappily. Trustfully.

Of course there had been an incident before, sometime in the early nineties. Some accusation or other. Molestation, probably. How that specific masturbation transpired, well, I'm not sure. That's when all this Wacko Jacko hoopla kicked into gear. Jokes proliferated. Everyone was a comedian all of a sudden. Some had questioned his eccentricities before, but mostly these peculiarities were written off as the excesses of celebrity. Wouldn't you want a roller coaster in your backyard? A pet chimp? But then that bedazzled hand searched a little too far out of the norm. His pop star fell so quickly. Suddenly he was a blanched black man with a fake face who liked to jostle the genitals of little boys. Jostle their genitals genially. Jostle their genitals germanely, generously, and gregariously.

At his Neverland Ranch, Peter Pan got underage Lost Boys drunk on what he called Jesus Juice and showed them porno. Supposedly. Jacko licked the boys' faces. That's what they're saying. He had outercourse with them and he masturbated them and was masturbated by them in a plethora of ways. According the reports from within the court, the Accuser would be able to identify the pop star's mottled, vitiligo-stricken penis from some sort of schlong line-up. The details are so peculiar that the heinousness of what may actually have transpired seems to have had all the gravity sapped from it.

All his eccentricities and social faux-pas he blames on his stardom. It's because he never had a childhood. It's because he was thrown into the biz by some brutal beast of a father, that he so craved the presence of children. No childhood? Oh, cry me a river.

Whatever the reasons, old Wacko Jacko is up to his old tricks. Dancing on top of cars and wearing pyjama pants to his molestation trial. And because cameras aren't allowed inside of the court house, some channels are airing dramatizations based on the transcripts. Jay Leno was subpoenaed but was able to cut a deal whereby he would still be able to make Wacko Jacko jokes on his late night talk show. Those gibes are his bread and butter.

Frivolously. Tangentially. Pithily. Conclusively. Mercilessly.
Concretely. Tenderly. Quizzically. Sweetly. Contradictorily. Whim-
sically. Superciliously. Partially. Severely. Mightily. Weakly. Ceaselessly. Blithely. Calmly. Mentally. Unbelievably. Poorly. Unsatis-
factorily. Sincerely. Tyrannically. Diplomatically. Cannibalistically.
Detrimentally.

Aimlessly the light washed steadily over the car.

As it happened, Janice was the same age as my older brother Greg
when she married my father. With wife #1 my father had Greg in
1966. That fell apart because both of them had relationships on
the side. The woman that my father had been wining and dining
became wife #2, birthing me in 1985. She ankled in 1994, and a
year later he married #3, the Head Archivist at the Corbet Public
Library, dying before he had a chance for a #4. Sara Plain-and-
Tall's homely best friend. A woman whose natural scent was boiled
cabbage. A woman the same age as his first son. A woman old
enough to be my sister.

Janice became a Fagel with two projects in mind. First, she set
about organizing my childhood that she had missed. That led grace-
fully into her next task, which was to ingratiate herself into my
heart, to cleave herself to little me.

Considering her archivist's sensibility, the first task was a cinch.
When handling anything, cotton gloves were a must. Emotionally,
mentally, socially, Janice wore cotton gloves. She always impressed
upon me the preciousness and fragility of life. To handle anything
in a careless way is to risk corrupting it. But she also actually would
wear cotton gloves sometimes, legitimately worried about how
corruptive the oils on her fingers could be. Rooting around in boxes
full of crappy pictures I had drawn, spelling tests that I had done
reasonably well on, Janice shook her head and muttered, "Your
mother must not have loved you at all. These boxes aren't even
acid-free."

The ingratiation was not so easy, mainly because it involved
me, my actual participation. My attitude at the time was complete

evasion. Janice read my reticence all wrong. She thought that I was hiding in my room the same way a wounded animal will slink into hiding to die. At first she thought I was still having difficulty dealing with the loss of my mother, and then the loss of my father, when really I just couldn't stand running into her, having to talk to her. Janice's solution was to insist that I enter myself in my grade school's talent night. That was sure to bring me out of my shell.

By then, Greg had been moved out of the house a few years and already took back his mother's maiden name. Janice was all there was.

She brought hardly any of her own furniture, seeming content to simply organize what was already there. Janice made my house not a lived-in home, but a stayed-in home, like a hotel room that is cleaned daily so that when you return it's as if you had never before been there. The one new item that she did introduce to my familiar surroundings was her own mother's upright piano, which she put in the corner of the den. The varnish was weathered and the keys were yellow from half a century of cigarettes. The sheet ledge was of course replete with Jackson's song books. With a shyness suggestive of guilty pleasures, Janice liked the funky, dancey aspects of his music—the early stuff—but when it came to the schmaltzy, maudlin ballads—starting with "Ben" and extending to that song from the "Free Willy" soundtrack—Janice was unabashed. Some nights she would plonk ceaselessly, in rounds, self-conscious of the sound of her own voice, so thinking the passionate lyrics in her head, to herself. Jackson—like Jesus, why no?—was out to heal the world, to make it a better place through song.

The song she chose for us to perform was "Heal the World" from the Dangerous album. The cover of the songbook—the proceeds of which went to Jackson's own Heal the World Foundation, which has recently gone bankrupt—showed a cracked earth with a chubby pink band-aid over the fracture. It was a call to loving arms, the song, a plea for help with ethereal synth strings and wind chimes.

With a glassy look, Janice described to me exactly how the

performance would go. In the darkness following the previous performance there would be excited chatter and some hooting. From out of this darkness the root chords would begin softly and, as the talking died down, Janice would begin adding notes until all attention was focused on the stage. Then I would be illuminated by the soft glow of the spotlight. (All of this she would arrange with the technicians.) With a tone of sadness I would enter the first verse, because, after all, the song is about the ills of the world, about hungry and hurt and dying children.

"Hurt is the lock," Janice explained. "And song is the key that opens up the lock of hurt that keeps us out of our own hearts."

Slowly, as I, accompanied by Janice, introduced my classmates to their own hearts through the sombre truths of the broken world, the tone would begin to brighten, the pace would quicken, because once we were all inside of our own hearts we would realize that joy and song in the presence of darkness is all it takes. Basically, the arc of the performance found everyone on their feet, clapping, stomping and singing along with me in the end, as I spun and twirled and slapped my knee. Janice wondered if my elementary school had a wind machine.

"And maybe the houselights could come up then, too. Because it's not just about you anymore. It's about the lot of us."

While she didn't include this in her description, I can imagine how the rest of Janice's fantasy went. As the song is taken over by the student body of Bogle Corbet Elementary, both me and Janice remove ourselves from the song. I step away from the microphone and she stands up from the piano, though the music is magically still playing. She comes to me as much as I come to her. And we embrace, there in the soft spot, as son and mother. The stomping, singing and clapping isn't necessarily for us, but it also sort of is. Because we have healed the world. We have made it a better place. Together. As our bodies squeeze close, that fracture is mended. They cheer. They all cheer. And we don't have to say anything.

That one month of rehearsal was the only time that Janice and I made things work. For two hours a night, gathered in the den around the piano, we were son and mother. The intensity of Janice's belief was beguiling, I'll admit. I believed every saccharine, hackneyed word. Maybe her faith in me, too, in my ability to move my peers to such action, helped. She assured me that my shy, wobbly voice was just fine and that, after all, the point isn't the medium, but the message. Confident, song spewed from my diaphragm, snapping and popping like ice in the spring.

If there was ever a time to say it or to have said it, right then was the only time I would have said I love you.

As soon as the first act took the stage that afternoon, I understood how egregiously I had been misled. Massively. With cardboard guitars and a drum kit made of Rubbermaid trash bins, the three toughest guys in school performed an air band to "Smells Like Teen Spirit." After not even a minute of lip synching and pretend strumming, they started to trash the stage, smashing their fake guitars and kicking in the garbage bins. The violence was permitted for only a minute more before The Bums were led off the stage by the principal, the crowd cheering them on. Passing me backstage, where I was tucking my golden blouse into my black slacks, and adjusting my shin guards, they shoved me and said, "Nice wig, fag."

Aside from a few earnest Asian students that, even though they played violin better than any of us would be able to do anything in our lives, hadn't even an ounce of stage presence, all the other acts were jokes. With choreography thrown together last minute, the other boys in my class pranced around and pretended to sing Billy Ray Cyrus, or Kriss Kross, or, in the case of obese and self-effacing Craig Lawson, Weird Al Yankovich's parody of Michael Jackson's "Bad", "I'm Fat."

"But you have to do it," Janice said, shocked and hurt, when I told her I was backing out. "We've worked so hard. Do it like we practiced and you'll be great. Remember the key. The hurt. Their hearts, Will."

Momentarily buoyed by Janice's assurances, I went through with it. At his podium, the principal introduced us. "Singing 'Heal the World' we have William Fagel, accompanied by his mother on the piano."

Just like she said, there was the darkness. Laughter in the dark. Fart noises in the dark. Chirps that sounded like "fag" in the dark. Then the root chords. All like she said. Except, jogged out of the trance Janice had put me under, I could hear her lack of rhythm, her missed notes. The spotlight came up on me, just like she had said, and my spangled glove twinkled. The oil in my curled wig glistened like a garbage bag lacquered in morning dew. I missed my cue in the uproar. Janice's poor piano playing was drowned out in the guffaws. Panicking, I jumped in, not in any sort of key.

Hearing me tell them about the place in their hearts called love, imploring them to heal the world they lived in, was enough. The laughter of my peers couldn't be stifled. No key that I knew of could open their hearts. Looking back, the next few years of my life would have maybe been salvaged had I rushed off stage and done my sobbing in the wings. Instead, I stayed, the microphone turning my blubbering and bawling enormous.

Oversimplification doesn't interest me. Generally, I don't believe that any trajectory in your life can be traced back to one specific launch pad. But all the same, that afternoon was it. From then on, I didn't trust Janice. Her views and opinions had nothing to do with the world that I wanted to live in, the world that most people lived in.

Had I not been so eager to live down my public weeping, maybe I wouldn't have been as willing to take the chances that I did. A month after Janice and I tried to heal the world, I rolled grass that had been sprayed with pesticide into some loose-leaf Hilroy paper, holding the joint together with tape, smoking it under tutelage of The Bums. Had my jaw been wired shut at the time, I don't doubt that I would have drowned in my own bile. No question.

The light was large and harsh and I had to open my eyes against it slowly. From sleeping with my head craned against the window all night I had a crick in my neck that hooked up into my head split-tingly. Our car was parked beside a gas pump and without having to move my head I could see directly into the convenience store, could see Janice—stooped, hair a mess and mouth hanging open a little—waiting in line to pay. However long she'd been gone, she'd left the windows rolled up and the car was stifling and fusty. Undeniably, from me, the smell of crotch. Hungover crotch. The tear-away pants I had been wearing all month did little to contain the stink.

Similarly, because of poor ventilation, my mouth was pasty, skuzzy. Things need to breathe or else they go rotten.

Feeling behind me, I caught the handle and swung the door open. Into the dry, staid air, I crab-walked, scooting and easing myself across the back seat. Looking up, hanging half out of the car, the sky was diluted and cloudless. The sun was high and soft at its edges like it wasn't quite noon, but almost. Successfully out and with my palms dappled by pebbles and glass, I lay by the pumps and breathed in the petrol fumes. Once or twice I'd consented to huff gas, but, that concentrated, the smell is too overwhelming, repugnant and thick. Ingratiated into the air is best, where it's ubiquitous and sweet. Salubrious even. Like a good woman, a good drug is one that is not demanding, but rather is complementary to your moods. Morphine is demanding, as I found in the hospital. Concentrated gas fumes are demanding to the extent that the nausea comes quick and settles itself in for the long haul. While a little is fine, too much cocaine is demanding, your thoughts become too many thoughts for you, the shepherd, to organize. They bleat and they rush and they scatter.

Like picking the right wine for your meal, you have to be smart about what you take when. Drugs wouldn't have such a bad rap, I don't think if it weren't for all the mindless goobers scarfing them rain or shine like they were going out of fashion. Drugs don't kill people, people do that to themselves. Guns don't kill people, assholes do. And, come to think of it, maybe Jackson wouldn't have wound up such a queer duck if it weren't for all those fanatics using him so recklessly. Maybe. Blame it on the boogie, why don't you.

Having inhaled fumes enough to soothe the crick, I took my

time standing and then ducked back into the car for my crutch and for the overnight bag Janice had packed me, where my mouthwash and peroxide were. On the hood of the car I set up the works. The fissures in the windshield were snaking closer, seeming to want so badly to touch, like the finger of Adam and his Maker.

In the larger Scope cap I mixed three parts hydrogen peroxide with one part mouthwash, swished it around for about two minutes until my cheeks began to strain and my stitches stopped stinging and spat into the squeegee bucket hung on the pillar. My surgeon couldn't stress enough how imperative keeping up this routine was, seeing as brushing and flossing were impossible. God forbid my mouth wounds become infected. Then I'd be in real bad shape.

Bearing four cups of coffee in a tray, Janice bummed the glass door open and came back out to the car. Shoulders high into a pensive hunch, Janice has always carried herself as if some loud clatter has just happened behind her and she's waiting for another report before turning to see what calamity has occurred. Never one to throw away anything, she saved all the clothes I had grown out of. And a penny pincher through and through, she wore all those old clothes of mine, was sporting them now. A bright blue sweatshirt with a cartoon ALF on it, making the a-okay sign with his fingers and saying "No Problem" and jeans from when I was eleven, rolled over twice at the cuffs.

Figuring out what my father saw in her is not rocket surgery. Unlike other divorced men in their early seventies, he had not married a fake-tittied gum snapper. Instead, he married a mom.

"Would you like a coffee?" she asked, setting the tray down on the hood.

I held up my cap and bore a metal smile. Like just before I shot, I toasted her.

"That's good. I was going to remind you." She folded the lid back onto itself and took a cautious little sip. "Are your stitches coming out yet?"

"Ittle its."

"Good."

She pushed her blocky glasses down to her nostrils and massaged the bridge of her nose, then worked her fingers into the corners of her eyes. She looked as bad or worse as I've ever looked in the throes of any lengthy trip. A day in, your head's still on the ride—or her big fat heart, in this case—but your body just wants to get off. Poor Janice, she was into this scene in a bad way. But that's her business. She never really said boo to me about my using so, as a favour, I'd butt out too, let her make her own mistakes. Let her drive two days straight to join the rest of the nut jobs rallying for Jackson outside the courthouse.

I pinched the armpit of my shirt and held it to my nose. A little too sour for anyone's good. Under a disapproving though polite glare from Janice I took it off and looked for another in my overnight. Finding nothing that suited my tastes, and feeling too hot and restrained anyhow, I let my concave belly show.

"Hour ou healing?"

"Tired. But we're just about there. Over half."

"Air're 'e?" Across from gas station was an empty plot of land, flaxen and barren except for a billboard, which was blank, selling us nothing.

"Nebraska."

Unable to wet my own lips, they were splitting terribly. I applied a greasy load of Vaseline.

"Ooks ike a lowly pace."

"Sorry?"

"Ooks ike a lowly pace," I said.

"I don't know what that means."

A day had passed, her and me together. Head airy from lack of sustenance and now the fumes, my enmity had diffused. Stuck in the same place with a person for that long, it's hard to maintain your ire. Anger can get to be a bore. But still. As with the itches, as soon as I remembered it, the sores flared.

"Ever mind," I said and walked around to the other side of the car, opening the door and laying myself back down. Janice basked in the bright, desolate landscape a moment more before getting back behind the wheel. Again she tilted the mirror to look at me.

"Are you sure you wouldn't rather ride up front with me?"

"S," I said. Her worried eyes pouted at me a second more and then turned away. She ignited the car and the tape flared up halfway through a song. Our song.

Yes, Michael, we really could get there if we cared enough for the living. You hit the nail on the head. Recalibrate our hearts and make it a better place, indeed. It's that simple. You've done a fine job of it, after all. It may come up in your trial that, in fact, outer-coarse, Jesus Juice and grandma porn all possess curative properties that will, in the end, heal the world

Janice pulled out and we found our way back onto the interstate, back into the doldrums.

Man, that itch. And that stink.

Frugally. Fiercely. Fugaciously. Figuratively. Frequently. Flippantly. Floridly. Fluently.

Driving through the prairies is like a cheap old cartoon where the background repeats on a loop and it feels as if you're moving but getting nowhere. You're on some cursed carousel at the worst fair in the world. Only, instead of calliope, Michael Jackson serenades you as you go around and around and around.

Convivially. Coarsely. Callously. Carousingly. Cacophonously.

The prairies are a bad memory that you're forced to repeat until, suddenly, you don't care anymore. You find yourself no longer so rankled, able to move on, and the prairies become the desert. Flaxen becomes sandy and then dun, and then becomes a little red. There's nothing in the windswept fields, then little humps of cacti which elongate, growing raised arms like it's a stick up. One cactus I saw had its arms stretched straight out, like a crucifix. Isn't that one of Michael Jackson's famous poses? Where he goes onto his toes, sticks both his arms out for balance and droops his head with a "Who!"

And sky. Always only sky ahead, until the hills and mountains that roll and curl like the sleeping bodies of scraggly stray tabby cats. Utah becomes Arizona, and then it's Nevada. There are hovels in the distance, roadside kiosks where Indians sell crafts and jerky. And then, all of a sudden, there's Vegas. A futuristic city surrounded by fallout and wasteland. Such lushness and excess built overtop of complete environmental squalour. Someone found that wilderness and said, I can overcome this. I can do better. All we can ever do is see something and either say, I don't want it, or I want it but different.

Vivaciously. Vitriolically. Vehemently. Vapidly. Voraciously. Vindictively.

Other motorists and passengers. We're all sneaking peaks into each other's vehicles. You look in at them and they're already looking out at you, droopy with interstate malaise. Bumper cars passing but bumping only glances. Or else you were the one staring without realizing it, and they're looking at you looking at them. Or it may just be that everyone's looking into everyone else's car, expecting to see someone looking. It's too subconscious a thing to know for sure. I tried to make a game of not looking up until the car was directly beside of us, but the problem is no different.

Capriciously. Convexly. Covetously.

Janice would tilt the mirror, find my eyes, and ask, "Are you hungry?"

"All wish," I would say.

After almost a month of being wired against most intake, my stomach shrank and the hunger became a sort of fullness. There's what our bodies actually need to function, and then there's the amount we actually eat, which is always decided—our hunger is decided—by how much we had to eat last time. Having had nothing to eat when we left, by the night of the second day, I needed less than nothing.

Conspicuously. Caringly. Mindfully.

Lucidity came in and went out like skateboarding. I'd rest my eyes, and after only a few winks, close my eyes and when I opened them back up the sun would be in a different place, or else it had fallen. I woke up once to the rumbling of interstate vertebrae beneath us and punched the back of Janice's seat. "Annish! Ache up!" She startled awake and righted our car.

"Geeshush."

I'd forget about my itches and as soon as I remembered them, they'd return.

Longitudinally. Lividly. Lithely. Listlessly. Languidly.

The morning we left I woke up to the wail of a vacuum, ready to die. In the bathroom I stood in front of the mirror, wire cutters in hand, waiting for the bile. When it didn't come I swished with hydrogen peroxide, spat out a spidery little stitch, and headed downstairs. In an attempt to offend Janice's sense of decency, I liked to move about the house in nothing but my underwear until usually five in the afternoon. Hopping down the stairs with the banister for support, I saw that the Dirt Devil was standing up at the landing, sucking at the same square of floor just beside the shoes. Janice was in the den watching the TV with the volume turned up loud enough to be heard over the vacuum, on the edge of the couch with her chin in her hands. On the coffee table, square and bulky like an apothecary's medicine bottle, was the empty bottle of Jager. Greg had sold me down the river.

On the TV, Michael Jackson was dancing on top of a black SUV—skinny and jittery like a marionette—despite reported back problems. All the channels had been running this clip for the past month.

She turned to me, a fingernail between her teeth. "Will," she said, pausing and frowning at my naked, hollow belly before turning back to the TV, "You've got ten minutes to get dressed. Then we're leaving."

She pointed at the TV. The camera was panning over the gathered crowd slowly, eventually settling and zooming in on an old woman wearing a pink cowboy hat cradling a homemade Michael Jackson doll in her arms.

"When Jesus was arrested," Janice started slowly, "and accused of crimes that he did not commit, his disciples pretended not to know him. Maybe. Maybe if they had stood up for him, said that they knew him, said that he was who he said he was and would do what he said he'd do, well, maybe things would have turned out differently."

My lip split when I smiled, and the broader I smiled, the worse my jaw ached. But I couldn't help it, the damage had been done. The crack spread.

"Did you want to see him dance?" the Grandma Cowgirl had asked. "I can make little Michael moon walk."

Cosmically. Quaintly. Secretively. Humbly. Righteously. Carefully. Carelessly. Obviously. Accidentally. Clandestinely. Easily. Reluctantly. Ethereally. Fundamentally. Magically. Predictably. Wistfully. Stoically. Earnestly. Unabashedly. Insouciantly. Salubriously. Quintessentially. Ambiguously. Obviously. Obliviously. Obliquely. Obtusely. Acutely. Benignly. Coquettishly. Limply. Lethargically. Morosely. Artistically. Anachronistically. Archaically. Indicatively. Uselessly. Heartily. Disparagingly. Magnanimously. Brutally. Predictably.

Bombastically.

Languidly my eyes would creep open from a nap and the first thing I'd see would be a bored, blank face staring right back at me, as dull and tired as me. Staring and being stared at.

"Are you hungry?"

"All wish."

We didn't need to phone ahead to know that there'd be no vacancies in Santa Maria. The media had taken the little California town. And sure as I was born, where there are news cameras, there will be yahoos. The well funded media had booked up the local hotels and the yahoos the motels, leaving no room in the many mangers for me and Janice. So we stopped a few miles up US-101 in Pismo Beach. Arriving just after two in the morning, we managed to snag a room at the Best Western Shore Cliff Lodge. Palatial and swank— and more a night than Janice was hoping to pay, though she could afford it—every room in Shore Cliff had a balcony with a view of the Pacific. There was an outdoor pool, a lounge, and a gazebo that looked off the sheer drop that gave the hotel its name. The plan was to wake early and drive into Santa Maria to catch Jackson's arrival.

Janice checked out as soon as we checked in, moaning little restless moans as she slept. My first order of business—even before I snooped around in her purse for the minibar key—was to raid the closet for coat hangers. To discourage theft, the wire frames were connected firmly to the bar and took considerable violence to free. Janice slept through the clinking and clattering and the eventual crash as I tore the whole bar right from its socket.

I put my cast up on our balcony's railing and leaned back in a sort of pre-congress slouch, finagling the hanger to suit my desperate purposes. Long and with a little curled claw at the end, I sent my line in, scratching the smaller symptoms of the greater malady that had been consistently just a few inches above my ankle all that time.

At the source of my agitation my line snagged on to something. Easing the coat hanger out of my cast, I came up with an unexpected and felicitous catch. Grey and slightly lavender, rolled tightly in a sandwich baggy, the smell of winter clothes that have been in a cedar chest for a few seasons, Greg must have stowed them away during his Jager visit, after I had passed out. Just over a gram of mushrooms.

From our balcony I could see the far off gazebo, alone on the jutting nose of the cliff. Janice would be up and rejuvenated in a few hours so there was no point in trying to fall asleep, especially since I had been doing nothing but napping for the past few days. Half strolling and half skipping with my crutch, I wandered back through the empty lobby and out the back, past the lounge chairs, past the pool, out to the gazebo. From the wooden bench I could make out only the water, just a little darker than the morning sky, with steely dunes raised by the light, salty breeze.

Dropping a coin in a jukebox, I slid a slim bulb through the slot between my teeth. I'm sure I made a sour, baby face at the bitter, powdery taste. Not so different than the aftertaste of that pigeon that hit me. The repugnant taste of shrooms I could always bypass by wolfing them down, chomping and swallowing, getting the hard part over with. Now I had to carefully introduce each shrivelled bit into my mouth and let the rancid thing rest on my tongue until it became soggy enough for me to swallow and not choke on.

Always Greg had come through for me. As young as thirteen I would linger outside of the Beer Store or the LCBO like some red light floozy and goad adults into buying booze for me and my friends, or for just me. More often than not, we'd get screwed over. "What?" the adult would say, climbing into his truck with our beer. "You gonna call the cops on me?" Unlike Janice, Greg knew that whatever I was dealing with after our dad's death had to be dealt with on my terms. He was good about buying for me and when he started scoring pot soon after his only advice was, "Just don't be an asshole about it."

Except, now, as each little hallucinogen dissolved in my mouth, the taste of Greg's intentions this time around became clearer, more bitter and scathing, like the mushrooms themselves.

If he did believe, like he said, that I had royally fucked up, then he must have stowed the drugs away as a sort of question. An option to fuck up again if I really wanted to. In my experience, there's not a goddamn thing you can say to a friend to unhook them from whatever line they're caught on. They've got to figure it out for themselves. Maybe all it will take is the smell of their own festering bedroom to have them try a week without pot. Or maybe it won't be until the cartilage in their nose is dissolved and collapses that they'll realize that there's something a little bent about the way they're living their lives, that they should take a break from snorting so much meth. I wouldn't go as far as to say that I was bent, or overindulged, but it did hurt to think that Greg thought that about me, considering I know and have seen how dire certain straits can actually get.

By the time three-quarters were down the hatch the sun was coming up behind me. I could see it on the water furthest out, transubstantiating the metal shades of the night into the more golden ones of morning. Mostly there were stems and crumbs left like the bottom of a bag of pretzels and I didn't feel up to the challenge of softening dregs. I took up my crutch and headed back.

Janice was awake, sitting on the edge of her bed, lacing up the same pair of cheap beige nurse's shoes that she's had for as long as I've known her. She had on a woman's golden blouse tucked into the neutral black pants of a backstage set mover. She was wearing my old shin guards from soccer, spray painted a glittery silver and the curly black wig she had tucked her own hair under made her look more like A.C. Slater from *Saved by the Bell* than Michael Jackson. I'd thought as much when she had first given it to me to wear for the talent show.

Shoe tied, she lifted her bum a little and pulled out from her back pocket one of her cotton archivist's gloves, which she had covered in sequins. She slid her hand into it with an elegance I'd never seen in Janice before.

The initial shock was hilarious, but the urge to laugh was quickly stifled by a breaker of intense revulsion and sadness. Like a best friend so high out of their tree that they say they'll eat dog shit. It's sidesplitting. But then they seriously start eating it. And then, without even a glimmer of humour in their face or tone, they say that you should too.

"Hokay," she said, smacking her thighs with finality. "Let's skedaddle."

Crudely, Janice had also managed to fix the broken bar in the closet.

The wacko's flocked. They flocked and then they flocculated, clumping and pushing against the links like it was just another one of his concerts. A law had been passed about climbing on the fence, so instead they brought stepladders to get a better view. Everyone tries to see over, to see through, to see past, and in between the human mess of other lookers, around the untanned cottage cheese calves of gawkers on their ladders, I could make out the Justice Centre. It was clean, white and modern with red clay tile roofing. Like most of what I'd seen of California so far, it looked brand new. Unsullied but for the litter of sheriffs, bailiffs, security guards, and reporters milling in front.

Between us and the main stage were the reporters, who were themselves penned off like cattle by bike racks, each one relegated to their own parking space on the Justice Centre's lot. Sending reports back to headquarters, to affiliates. The neighbourhood was teeming, the surrounding houses all commandeered. The residents must be getting rich off this trial. There were news vans parked in the driveways, reporters and spectators on the tiled roofs and satellite dishes erected in the backyards next to over turned swing sets. Sending signals out all around the wounded earth, spreading the word either like ointment or like salt, depending on who you asked.

"You should have been here earlier, for the lottery," a three-hundred-pound Puerto Rican man dressed in shades and an ill-fitting red leather Thriller jacket told us. He had a stroller in front of him, with a limp, sleeping daughter inside, under the shade of the awning. His own face was round and smooth like a baby's. A little glum and tired, though he appeared gleeful in his weariness. Gleefully weary. Ebulliently weary. Triumphantly weary.

"The lottery?" Janice asked.

"For public seating inside the courthouse. They only let the *Irish* in today." His little girl pawed languidly at the air with a yawn and then collapsed back to her impotence. "It thinned out for a while then, but when he's coming in and when he's leaving is when it gets really nutso-cuckoo. After nine you can tell who's out here for the right reasons." The gathering was thin, but gaining numbers. With a dog at the end of a leash a jogger ran on the spot while taking a look, before thumping away again. Teenagers wandered in and took pictures with their cellphones, before giggling on down the road. A red-faced, sun-hardened derelict conducted interviews with an empty fist, while the real media, trying to be as inconspicuous as possible, gathered scoops and personal interest stories, or else raised their camera for a shot then lowered it quickly to their side, not wanting to draw too much attention to themselves. A few people in the crowed stood as if lost, looking around them trying to recognize their surroundings, like they had woken up in the sea of people with no explanation, no recollection of how they got there. "Some of us have been here all along."

Janice nodded with intense agreement. She nodded intensely. She nodded knowingly, vehemently, credulously. The tulip had finally found the right sun, and was opening up its face to the weird beams. Her posture seemed to improve and though I couldn't see her eyes behind her aviator glasses, I'm sure they must have been twinkling. Twinkling brightly.

Just before eight in the morning the smell was of scorched flesh, of cooked sodium, met with the beach towel wafts of sunscreen and the stiff medicinal fogs drifting over the crowd from the reporters' hairspray. Thriller said he'd been out there for days and sure enough he smelt like it.

Thriller sauntered away with his child, joining his group further down the fence.

Janice and I were a few bodies back from the barrier. Wading through, we passed the prayer circles: held hands, bowed heads, and sombre, quiet hallelujahs. There were prayers both for and against Jackson, of course. On the sidewalk across the street were the hollering godheads. One big bear of a man waved a sign aloft that read "The SHED BLOOD of JESUS CHRIST MAN'S ONLY SALVATION." I couldn't tell which side of the People v. Jackson divide he was on. The devotees had let me gimp passed, respectfully and a little jealously, taking me for some terminally ill child come to have Jackson's healing hand placed on his feverish head maybe. And Janice, all Jacksoned-up, enjoyed a certain priority. They seemed to want the more garish followers in the foreground, as a show of even greater support. Every one of them willing to step in for Jackson at any moment, to take the heat. How easy would it have been for Christ to slip away into the gathering of beards, to be replaced by a willing fan? Fairly.

He was all there, all of him from every epoch. Everywhere you turned. There was a dwarf playing young Michael, sporting a grand afro and florid poncho. Though I'm not sure whether the nine-year-old ingénue smoked such large cigars or cursed so much. A little ways down from his younger self was the young king of disco, broken out of the Jackson 5 and on his own. A young man on the make, the afro was smaller and the white, flared suit was classy but still workable on the dance floor. He was holding a sign that said "BLAME IT ON THE BOOGIE." And I was pretty sure he was a woman. In fact, most of the believable doppelgangers appeared to be women. Even Janice pulled off her costume better than the Thriller, or the other grown men whose bellies showed under their red leather jackets. Like baby's gurgling beneath their mobiles, the adults seemed to be pawing for some whirling perfection that's always just out of reach. Pawing at the whirling perfection hungrily. Happily pawing. Gladly pawing.

"What's *your* deal?" A mid-'90's Jackson sidled between us, but addressed me. He was a lanky she in black-face, wearing black slacks ankle high, showing off pristine white socks, a broad-brimmed hat and white glove like Janice's, bandages on both wrists and a white v-neck undershirt that showed her mosquito bites and had yellow stains in the armpits. Her sign said "Sneddon BEAT IT!" Mirrored aviator glasses hid her eyes and reflected back at me my own face. After a month, I'm still a little shocked when I catch a look at myself. Like Janice, maybe, I still harbour a young face in my mind. I forget how twisted my mug is now: raccoon circles around my eyes the brown and yellow colour of a bruised banana, thick and swollen nose, walrus jowls, and dry, cracked lips that are puckered into a gritty metal grimace.

"Um ear do be eeled," I muttered vacantly, deadly, fixated instead on my own face, trying to recognize bygone features.

The woman's face took on a sudden glaze of disdain, like she could smell the snark on me. Like in Peter Pan, all the children of the world needed to clap, needed wholeheartedly believe in fairies if Jackson was to beat the rap. The disbelieving hands of snicker-pusses could screw the whole charm. When she turned to Janice, a true believer, the enmity left her, replaced by a smile unnaturally big.

"You're new?" she asked, taking Janice's gloved hand in her gloved hand.

"We just came in this morning."

"Canadian?"

"We are."

"Jeez. That's super." With the consistency of the metronome atop Janice's piano, the woman continued to shake. "It's our own little world here. I've been here all along and I've met supporters that have come out from places not even listed on any maps. I tell ya. The way the media would have you believe, we're a race at each other's throats. And I won't lie and say that I didn't believe it. I did until I got out here and saw just how able all of us are to come together in tough times like these. It's not us that's sick. It's those vipers." Saying this, the woman finally left Janice's hand free and pointed to one of the cameramen filming a little Jackson 5 down the row. "They twist. They alter the truth. They decide how we will see the world."

"Well," Janice said. "We've been watching on TV. I felt so helpless, so useless at home. I just had to come out."

"That's it exactly. That's the way they make you feel exactly: useless. You forget how much power we actually have to make this world a better place. Have you got a sign?"

The derelict wandered into our circle. Other than his scrofulous grey beard and greening jeans with a large hole ripped out of the seat, he seemed to have his wits about him completely. He stuck his empty fist into this woman's face, this woman who more and more seemed to have made herself leader of the doppelgangers.

"Do you feel that you've had a fair trial so far?" The old man's voice was clear, he enunciated as well as any anchorman.

"Would you scram, Ben? Huh?" Again disdain curled her lip, curled it cruelly. Curled it hatefully.

"What do you mean a sign?" Janice asked.

His hollow hand found its way just under Janice's lips, like he was holding an ice cream cone for her to nibble at. "Do you think your public image will ever recover?"

"Um."

"Jesus, Ben … Take a hike. Okay?" Again the leader's ire was showing through her cosmetics, like a whitehead that refuses to be muted by concealer. "A sign like mine. Did you bring one?"

"No. I guess I didn't think to."

The reporter turned to me now. His eyes were cloudless and blue as the prairie skies. Intense and careful. "Did he do this to you, son?"

The leader's hands were at her hips now, her dancing shoe tapping impatiently. Tapping perturbedly. Tapping tunelessly. The skin on my lips opened at the broadness of my initial smile. The dry hurt came at the same time as another sort of pain. Affected and worried, my interviewer's eyes. Their earnestness made my snarky smile feel suddenly very ugly, very out of place. Callous. "Is this his doing?" he asked again, deadpan, respectfully. "You can tell me."

A homely man with a face roughly hewn by circumstances, the more I looked at him, looked a little into him, I could see that his intentions were handsome, dashing. A genuinely good person. A genuinely confused person that very much wanted to get to the bottom of this travesty. A genuine person amidst the costumed.

"Son?"

I leaned forward and spoke as clearly as I could into the emptiness of his fist, round like the world. "Yesh," I said. "It wash him."

He put his other hand softly on my shoulder. Given the time, I could have surly let a few tears fall. But Jackson had had enough.

"For fuck sake's, Ben. Would you piss off already!" She shoved him hard at the shoulder. Ben, not expecting it, stumbled back and onto the ground. He held up the hand that had just held his microphone and regarded the angry red scrape. Then showed it to us before trundling back into the crowd, which was becoming denser now. Behind her mirrors, Jackson rolled her eyes. "I'll go get you a sign."

Turning to Janice, I looked for some shimmer of disapproval

but was met only by my own hurt look in her eyes.

"I want to go," I said, my lips overworking like a fish at the surface of its fishbowl, kissing at its flaky dinner. Thoughtfully Janice pouted her bottom lip and took my elbow in her sparkling hand with confidence and intention. She never touched me. Maybe then she would have said something, finally, even if it was "Up your nose with a rubber hose, you brat, we're staying put," but was nudged forcefully from behind. She stumbled and then fell into me, sending me to the ground. A wail from some girl and then the applause of shutters opening and closing.

Bodies swarmed us while Janice helped me to my feet and back onto my crutch. The black SUV pulled up to the courthouse.

The agitated mass blocked my clear view of Jackson. He was a little body shuffling between two hulking bodyguards, one of whom was holding a parasol over him. Attendant for the King. The imitators rattled the links, wanting hungrily to burst free. All of him slavered and howled, some of him crying. Shouts of encouragement and condemnation.

And then Jackson turned. He looked over his shoulder and waved a dainty little wave at all of his fans, at his disciples, at his lost boys.

Of course I've been seeing images of his face all summer long, but for that split second it struck me. What a mess this man has become. A sallow, hollowed out, pallid face, destroyed by so much expensive tinkering. His gait was unsure, supported. He is so changed, so unrecognizable from the person he once was. On the other side of the fence are his prime, his excellence, his youth. His image has remained unsullied, unaged, while he himself has absorbed all the hideousness of his excess. He is Dorian Gray's portrait.

Janice had to have seen this, too.

From down the line came a loud "Sha-mon!" Everyone turned to look. The Head Jackson, the one we had just been hectored by, had now knocked a reporter's camera to the ground and was engaged in a flurry of hand chops, knee slaps, and foot kicks. There was the occasional groin grab and awkward exhalations of "Who?

Who?" and "He! He!" The cameraman was confused and a little frightened, but once he regained his senses, he laid the woman out with one punch. When we turned back, Jackson was gone.

"I'm sorry," Janice said. She removed her glasses and looked at me blatantly, her eyes small and sullen and swollen. Not worried like usual, not searching for her lost boy in a crowded supermarket, but just tired. "This was a bad idea."

The morning sun illuminated the soft hairs on her face, giving her a warm glow. Very slightly her face shifted, took on weight, took on the moroseness of intelligence brought on by dejection and age. Janice wilted and bloomed simultaneously. She changed in my eyes. In my eyes she changed.

"Oh shit, Sherlock," was all I said. All I had to say. All she deserved.

Other than the new one I made up along the way—the one with the adverbs—the only other driving game I have ever played is punch buggy. The object is to be the first player to spot a VW Bug on the road. Your prize is that you get to punch your opponent on the shoulder. Whether hard or soft, that's entirely up to you.

The summer before his aneurysm, my father packed family #3 into this same inclement-day-blue Civic and lit out for Point Pelee. I was eleven then. His hope must have been that sequestering me with Janice in a sweaty car for four hours along the 401 would break me, would force me to bond with her. From the front passenger seat Janice suggested a game, maybe, to help the time fly. Punch buggy, I said. We spotted the same Bug in tandem, only I acted quicker. As she turned to point it out, my punch was already in the mail. Signed, sealed, and posted.

With vigour I missed her shoulder by a mile and clocked my brand new stepmother square in the jaw.

The hit to her face was so obviously accidental—and afterwards I was so gushingly apologetic, so embarrassingly apologetic, so contritely apologetic—that neither my father or Janice thought to ask, regardless of whether I was actually aiming for her face or not, why I had meant to hit her so hard on the arm.

Andrew Hood

ESPLANADE
Books

THE FICTION SERIES AT VÉHICULE PRESS

[Andrew Steinmetz, editor]

A House by the Sea
A novel by Sikeena Karmali

A Short Journey by Car
Stories by Liam Durcan

Seventeen Tomatoes: Tales from Kashmir
Stories by Jaspreet Singh

Garbage Head
A novel by Christopher Willard

The Rent Collector
A novel by B. Glen Rotchin

Dead Man's Float
A novel by Nicholas Maes

Optique
Stories by Clayton Bailey

Out of Cleveland
Stories by Lolette Kuby

Pardon Our Monsters
Stories by Andrew Hood

Véhicule Press
www.vehiculepress.com